The Outcast Prince
and
the Cursed Princess

BEN HALL

Joshua Tree Publishing

• Chicago •

The Outcast Prince and the Cursed Princess

BEN HALL

Published by
Joshua Tree Publishing
• Chicago •
JoshuaTreePublishing.com

13-Digit Print ISBN: 978-1-956823-43-1
13-Digit eBook ISBN: 978-1-956823-51-6

Cover Image and Map Credit: Patrick Gatewood

Disclaimer:
This is a work of fiction. Names, characters, places, and incidents are the product of the author's imagination or have been used fictitiously. Any resemblance to actual persons, living or dead, events, locales or organizations is entirely coincidental.

Printed in the United States of America

DEDICATION

To Cheryl,
a truer friend
I couldn't ask for.

Map by Patrick Gatewood

CHAPTER 1

Noble Nominious slammed the great door to the king's chamber. *Just who does he think he is to oppose me?* he thought. As the head of one of the five leading houses that ruled over the southern half of the Island of the Mighty, House Nominious stood ideologically opposed to House Sovans, where King Leotan came from.

Strangling his cane, he stood shaking outside the throne room before darting off down a side hallway.

"That sovereign sissy thinks he can stop my house's progress," he said out loud, not caring who was listening. "It's time he learned that even kings aren't untouchable."

Rounding a corner, he collided with a thirteen-year-old boy who was making his way to his father's chambers.

"You shouldn't say such things about your sovereign," Prince Royce said.

"Are you speaking to me, *boy*? When you address your betters, you address them by their title or not at all, but perhaps I expect too much from a whelp of House Sovans."

"I am Prince Royce, my father is your king, and *you,* sir, would do well to remember *your* place."

The tip of Noble Nominious's cane whipped forward and pinned Royce to the wall.

"You arrogant little snot. I will not be lectured by the refuse offspring of a degenerate king."

Royce whimpered and squirmed, and just as he managed to twist his body and free himself, the noble thrust his cane between his feet, sending Royce to the ground. Kneeling on top of the prince, he brought his face in close.

"When I take the throne—"

The noble's eyes fluttered as he froze. Gasping, Royce pushed the noble off his chest and struggled to his feet. Prince Royce looked down at the pool of blood that was forming under the noble's chin from where the handle of the prince's ceremonial dagger extended. The exchange had not gone unnoticed, and as members of the Royal Guard rushed forward, Prince Royce ran for his life.

* * *

Two days had gone by since the death of Noble Nominious, and the houses were in an uproar. The prince had been confined to his quarters, and a guard was posted outside his room.

"King Leotan, respectfully, your son belongs in the dungeon, not in his bed chamber. The nature of his crime is most severe," the Bastion of Belthane said, to the surprise of many. The Island of the Mighty was divided in half, with the great river Kerberos running between the northern and southern continents. The northern kingdom was an impoverished and underdeveloped land, while the southern kingdom exuded prosperity. The southern realms were divided like a pie, with the capitol in the center, House Nominious to the west, and Belthane in the east, bordered by the great river Kerberos.

The land of House Dular lay between four realms at the southern end of the island. Immediately to their west, between them and Nominious, was the small realm of Kastlet, whose citizens were mostly fishermen. On their opposite side lay the lands of the Sovans, which boarders the Belthanes to the north.

Some argue that the Sovans and Belthanes were the strongest of allies. Others would insist that the friendship between House Nominious and House Dular was not to be underestimated.

"My son will stand trial for his crimes, and justice will be upheld."

"Then throw him in the dungeon," said Brassmas, acting head of the House Nominious. "Your son is accused of murdering my brother, the penalty for which is a swift and public execution. Our house demands that he be treated in accordance with these accusations as any other criminal would be if he weren't your son."

The chancellor stamped his staff numerous times as he shouted for order, though not for lack of being heard. From his perch in the far corner of the room, the acoustics echoed his every word to the overcrowded assembly. Never in the history of the land had something so atrocious occurred. The enormous turnout for the preliminary hearing was unprecedented.

As Brassmas took his seat, a messenger ran up to him.

"We can confirm that the prince is in the westernmost chamber of the family wing and guarded only by one guard. He will be receiving his evening meal promptly at six. You were correct in suspecting that the day's chef was supposed to be from our house, but late last night, he was replaced with one from the House Dular."

"That's no surprise," Brassmas told his messenger. "Now I have a message you must deliver to the Duke of Dular without delay. If anyone interferes with you in any way, you are authorized to use any means necessary to deal with them."

As the messenger hurried away, Noble Brassmas allowed himself a brief smile of satisfaction. *There was more than one way to get justice,* he thought.

* * *

Promptly at six, a commotion was heard just around the corner from the prince's room, followed by quick footsteps. The guard relaxed the grip on his sword upon seeing a lone servant carrying a tray toward him. However, as the servant drew near, recognition dawned in the guard's eyes.

"My Lord, why are you dressed up as—"

A savage uppercut snapped the guard's head backward before kneeling to place the food tray alongside the body. Removing a cloth from his waistcoat, he poured liquid onto it before entering the prince's chambers.

Stealing across the room to where the prince sat reading, the imposter placed the cloth over his nose and mouth. Following a brief struggle, the boy collapsed. The imposter wrapped, then tied the prince in his bed sheets and climbed down with him to a waiting carriage.

Making sure the prince could breathe, he covered him with a tarp and raced from the capital to the distant shore where a boat was waiting.

CHAPTER 2

“No one can know that I was here," Ivan Sovans said as he wearily walked through the door of Yao's house. Dawn was only a few hours away, and he had rowed all night to get to the Island of the Yaoites. A tall, strong man by most standards, his usually immaculate beard and mustache hadn't been groomed recently. Nor would they likely be soon, as he would begin the return journey back to the capital before his absence was noticed.

The only other person in the room was the clan's patriarch, a solidly built man in his mid-forties, the commander in chief of the warriors who bore his name. Among the most skilled and fiercest fighters in all of Nom, the Yaoites were swords for hire, masquerading as a community of farmers and fishermen living on one of the small islands just to the east of the Island of the Mighty.

"Just what are you involved in, Earl Ivan?"

"There have been complications at the castle," Ivan began. As he relayed the recent events involving his nephew, he concluded, "I realize this puts you in an impossible position. But if I may remind you, our house has gone to great lengths to ensure your nighttime activities remain anonymous. ”

"Activities that, I seem to recall, served the interests of the great House of Sovans," countered Yao.

"This is true," Ivan said as Yao's wife Cinthia entered and served them tea.

"What counsel do you offer, wife of mine?"

"What are we talking about?"

"Do not play childish games, woman. The wife of Yao is revered and feared for her quick wit and sharp tongue, so when I beseech her counsel among matters of men, she suddenly becomes a meek and timid schoolgirl and feigns that she hasn't been listening to the entirety of our conversation? I think not," Yao said.

"Does our esteemed guest propose sheltering the most wanted person in his kingdom will somehow equate to covering services that we have performed on behalf of his house? Would this not place him and his great house in our eternal debt?"

"Lady Cinthia makes a fair point," Ivan said.

"Ha, 'Lady,' he calls me. I am no frilly lady. I am the warrior maiden of my lord Yao who is permitted to give counsel among men. The wife of Yao is an honor no other woman can claim, and those who have tried have met with a swift death at my hand."

Ivan shifted uncomfortably in his seat and silently sipped his tea.

"Royce will need a new name," Cinthia said, leaving the room.

"Your wife makes valid points," Ivan replied, "and she is correct, of course, that the House of Sovans will eternally be in your debt."

"Now for a new name," Yao said, taking a long look into his tea for the answer.

"No, do not tell me. It's best that I don't know," Ivan said, rising and stretching his long limbs as the first hint of morning light competed against the brightness of the fireplace.

Royce woke to find himself lying on an ox skin in a strange little hut. As he struggled to identify his surroundings, a boy slightly older than he walked into the room and roughly set down a glass of water.

"Where am I, and where is Giovanni?" Royce demanded.

"You are in my house, and I don't know who Giovanni is."

"How dare you answer me so disrespectfully? You are dismissed. Maybe you should have thought about who you were talking to before you answered so rudely," he said as he made a wobbly attempt to stand. To his annoyance, the boy just stood there smirking at him.

"I said you are dismissed," Royce said, raising his hand. Moments later, he woke again with a vague memory that the boy had knocked him across the room. As he made his way to the door, he stared at lush green grass and sand so white it hurt his eyes.

"Roe quit standing around and go to the hall and help the cook with dinner."

Turning, he saw a woman walking toward him, carrying a basket of melons.

"And take these to him. He is expecting you. Well, what are you doing just standing there? Get going!"

Setting the basket on the ground, Royce said, "Lady, I don't know who you think I am, but I am not your slave. My name is—"

A swift slap across his face quickly silenced him.

"*My* name is Cinthia, and when I tell you something to do, you do it. When I tell you that your name is Roe, your name is Roe. Is that understood? Good, now take this basket to the big building over there with the smoke rising from it. Do you understand, or do you need me to explain it to you again?" she asked, leaning over him.

Royce bit back tears, holding a hand to the side of his stinging face. Picking up the basket, he made his way to the kitchen. Upon arriving, he saw one of the ugliest people he had ever seen hopping and dancing around the kitchen. The room was not like any kitchen he had ever imagined, but he had to admit he had never seen a kitchen. His meals were always brought to him.

The room only had three walls, and where the fourth wall should have been, there was a large brick oven at the ground level with three kilns opening at the height of his shoulders. He set the basket on the counter and found himself face-to-face with the cook.

"No, no, no! You never put the fruit where the fish is being cut up! Who taught you that?" the cook asked, scratching his head. "Name's Wuji, and I can see we have ourselves a long way to go. This is a harsh land we live on, and if you want to stay alive, then you had better be careful to do exactly what I say. Now see those jugs? They'd better be filled with fresh spring water when I return."

CHAPTER 3

"And why do we attack at night instead of at first morning light?"

"We attack at night only when we attack a larger foe. The cover of darkness allows us to escape our enemies. If we were to attack at first light, it would be a battle we believed we could win, and we would use the full light of day to ensure our victory."

From the canvas he hid under, Royce watched the man everyone called Yao question the boy that had brought him some water before knocking him out.

"And why are you going this night instead of last night or tomorrow?"

"We are going tonight because, as the lunar cycle tells us, tonight is the night of the full moon. And on the nights of the full moon, the ship-killing creatures avoid the surface."

While Royce had served dinner, he had come to learn that the boy's name was June. He wanted to be sure and remember as many names as possible for when his father came with the Royal Navy and rescued him.

"Since you are attacking on the night of a full moon, what's to prevent the enemies from observing your approach to their island?"

"The enemy will not observe our arrival because the color of our clothes matches that of the waves. Our sea craft is in four sections connected by strong ropes so that each section rides the waves independently of the other sections and masks our approach."

"Very good, June. As this is your first mission, either come back having destroyed the chieftain's house or don't come back at all. It makes no difference to me. I have no use for weak warriors."

As Yao turned away, he turned back and said, "I now enjoin you to the code of silence," and was gone.

Wordlessly June checked his short sword and recurved bow before getting into his boat. Royce had never seen boats like these before. Each held a single rower with two giant shells: the larger one they sat in and the smaller provided cover overhead. Four bamboo posts separated the shells. The boats were connected by a thick rope, both to mimic the motion of the waves and, from what he heard, if several members of the raiding party fell, all they needed was one to survive to get the rest home.

Attached to the four boats was a fifth that held four caskets of a sweet sticky substance that apparently was very flammable. Royce had just managed to conceal himself among the casks when Yao had approached and began questioning June. Wherever they were going, this was his chance to leave the island and reunite with his family. Then these people would pay.

As the party departed, no sound could be heard from the oars dipping into the water or from the raiders. The journey seemed to take hours until he heard voices off in the distance. As they grew closer, Royce guessed this would be as good a time as any to leave the safety of his boat and risk the attention of the night creatures that moved in the deep.

No sooner had he slid into the water than something bumped into his feet, traveling at a rapid speed underneath him. Panicked, he swam as fast as he could towards the beach, sure that he had been spotted by the guys in the boat. As soon as he gained the beach, he ran for his life into the jungle.

Sliding beneath the outstretching leaves of a tree, he watched as June, and his raiders silently hurried past him with the casks strapped to their backs. *Now what?* he wondered as the evening slowly passed. A flapping overhead revealed a leathery winged creature with an extremely long tail hovering just above his hiding place, and he couldn't be sure, but was it watching him?

Several moments later, he heard a cry of alarm off in the distance, and looking in that direction, he could see four men dressed in deep sea blue running towards the beach. A cry behind him startled him as he spun to see one of the islanders had snuck up on his hiding place. When June had passed by, the islander made a bird call before charging after the raiders. The call was answered, and several of the islanders joined the pursuit.

Royce glanced at the beach and saw the arrows peeking off the shell tops as the raiders peddled off into the night. He headed deeper into the jungle, but a flapping sound told him he was not alone. Nearing the other end of the trees, he saw a glow coming from a large house. Emerging from the jungle, he saw a man who appeared to be in charge. As he approached him, he heard a cry and was immediately surrounded by spears.

"My name is Royce Sovans, and I am the son of Leotan Sovans, sovereign of the Island of the Mighty. Return me to my father, and you will be greatly rewarded."

The men blankly stared at him, but with a gesture from their leader, he was tackled, bound, and gaged.

Chapter 4

As the sun rose, Royce sat in a cramped bamboo cage that was permeated with the smell of wet grass, smoke from a smoldering stalk beside his cage, and human excrement. He longed to stretch out, but the roof was only about waist-high, and the cell was as wide as it was tall. The men of the tribe would often walk by, poke him with long sticks, and yell at him in their language.

As the sun became hotter, Royce's stomach began to grumble. He had managed to get a little nap just before the door of his cage flung open, and he was dragged out by his feet before the chief. The men began yelling and poking him again, but every time he tried to stand, they would knock him back down. After several minutes, they dragged him back to the cage.

"The Sardiuses want to know why your friends left you behind."

Royce fixed his one eye that wasn't swollen shut on the old man in the cage next to his.

"I didn't do anything to them," he said through his split lip.

"They think you did because you wear the same clothes as the people who set fire to their chief's house. Just how did you come to be here?"

"I didn't do that, that was June, and he kidnapped me, but I got away."

"June, huh? I guess they finally made him a leader. Good for him," the old man said.

"These people can't do this to me; I am the son of a sovereign."

"Well, clearly they can, and it's probably a good thing that they don't understand you, or else they would hold you for ransom."

"That must have been what that guy Yao was doing with me," Royce said.

"Not sure I agree. I don't think Yao is the kidnapping and ransom type."

"Shows what you know. They took me from my home and made me their slave," Royce said before convulsing in coughs. The wind had changed directions, and now the smoke was blowing into his cage. Royce strained through the bamboo bars, grabbed the smoking stalk, and urinated on it to put out the embers. Moments later, another islander came by to yell at him and poke him. He threw the stalk in the man's face, grabbed the pole when it was dropped, and shoved the pointy end as hard as he could into the man.

"You shouldn't have done that," the old man said, scooting closer to the smoldering stalk next to his cage.

"Maybe you just want to sit there and get beat, but I am not you," Royce said, looking with satisfaction at the blood on the tip of the pole.

"No, I mean that you shouldn't have put out the smoking stalk. It was there for your protection."

Moments later, Royce heard the familiar sound of flapping leather wings as the creature with the long tail flew into his cage.

"Keep away from that thing, boy! You don't know anything about those creatures."

"It's all right. I met one like it last night in the jungle. They are harmless."

"They are attracted to outsiders. They leave the locals alone, but they hunt everybody else. I am warning you, keep away from its tail."

"You don't know what you are talking—*AAAAH!*" Royce looked down at a barb sticking out of his chest. The old man reached through his cage, grabbed the smoldering stalk, and brought it over to where Royce lay. The creature hissed at the fumes and flew away.

"You aren't going to die right away, but the next few weeks are going to be hell on you," the old man said, reaching through the poles and plucking out the barb, causing green poison to ooze from the wound.

As the sun set, there was a commotion among the islanders, who appeared to be under attack. Royce weakly watched as a body crashed into his cage and lay motionless. He was too weak to try and get to the man's weapon, so he just helplessly watched. He struggled to understand that the islanders weren't attacked by a rival clan; they were attacked by just one powerfully built man. The old man next to him began laughing when he noticed this also.

The lone warrior carried no weapon and faced about two dozen armed Sardiuses. The closest ones swung at him, but as he deftly avoided their attacks, he took their weapons from them and impaled them. Several of the Sardiuses launched their spears, and the warrior grabbed the first one out of the air and spun it to avoid the others before impaling the sender with his own weapon.

The chieftain observing this yelled a command, and the remaining Sardiuses dropped their weapons as they charged the lone warrior with their fists raised. A rapid succession of kicks and punches fell the first five, and when the remaining Sardiuses hesitated, the warrior charged them with a mighty yell. The battle moved out of Royce's view, but a short time later, the warrior appeared at their cage.

"Yao!" the old man said, laughing. Yao seemed to freeze as he regarded the old man for a moment.

"Brother of Yao's wife, we thought you were lost to us. How is it that you came to be captured?"

"I, too, thought I was dead, but then I woke in this cage," the old man said as Yao broke his cage open. Motioning towards Royce, he continued, "But the mighty Yao didn't leave his clan behind and journey here for me. That must mean this boy is who he claims to be."

As Yao broke open Royce's cage, he gently pulled him out. Examining his wounds, he washed them from his flask and then produced a salve, beginning to carefully treat him.

"I apologize for the misfortune you have undergone, young sir. The islanders blamed you for June's attack."

The last thing Royce saw was Yao's face as darkness claimed him.

CHAPTER 5

Royce woke and watched as Wuji placed a pungent-smelling bulb momentarily in a pot of boiling water. After removing it, he gently separated the bulb by its rings. Placing the even number of rings to one side, he layered the odd numbers with strips of thinly sliced salty meat before doing the same with the even number of rings, ending up with bulb ring, meat strip, bulb ring, meat strip, bulb ring, and leaving the center open. Arranging the bulbs cup-side down on a wire rack, he inserted them into the middle kiln and pulled a string on a hanging bag of sand, which began to slowly drain.

"There we go. By the time the bag is empty, the cooking will be done."

"What was that?" Royce asked.

"That? That was Yao's favorite breakfast. Once they cool, we place them in a clay pot and seal it up. Tomorrow, we will remove them from the pot, place them cup-side up on a skillet, crack an egg into the middle, and place them into the kiln for a few moments until the egg is finished."

"What other things does Yao like?" Royce asked as he pulled himself up.

"What's that now?"

"I mean, what are his favorite weapons? How did he become the Yao? Actually, never mind the weapons; I already know he doesn't use any. Where did he learn to fight like that?"

"Well, somebody has had a change of heart. Feeling better, are we?" Wuji asked as he diced some plant leaves.

"Who is Yao's favorite disciple? I'll bet it's June. What do I have to do to become a leader? I bet I can take June; he isn't much older than I am."

"Well, here comes the person who can tell you all about Yao," Wuji said, motioning to the lady heading towards them carrying a basket of large leaves. Royce scowled, recognizing Cinthia.

Entering the kitchen, Cinthia placed her basket down and watched Royce walk across the room to the large water pot.

"Well, it looks like Roe is finally up on his feet. About time he starts pulling his weight around here."

"For the last time, my name is Royce, you ignorant lady. Try not to forget it."

Within three quick steps, Cinthia crossed the room and smacked Royce across his face. Undaunted, Royce continued.

"You kidnapped and forced me to be your slave, but you will call me by my rightful name."

"Got a stubborn streak in you, huh? We'll see about that," Cinthia said, slapping him across the other cheek.

Royce grabbed a bowl of hot chili seeds and threw them in her face. As she screamed, he picked up the roller Wuji used for the dough but just as he pulled back and aimed for her head, Wuji snatched it out of his hand.

"Attacking Yao's wife is the quickest way to get yourself killed," he cautioned.

Splashing water across her face, Cinthia commanded Royce to sit.

"Just what is it that you think you are doing here?"

"You people kidnapped me!" Royce glared, refusing to sit down.

"That's where you are wrong. It was actually your uncle Ivan that brought you to us following your murder of the noble," Cinthia said, applying cream to her swollen face.

"Now you think of yourself as an intelligent young man. Do you truly believe that you could have gotten away with murder?"

"He attacked me! He slandered the king! That is something that people get banished for but not the Noble of Nominious. He can run his mouth any time he wants without consequences."

"And since this is true of the noble, what do you think that means for someone who doesn't have any power? Someone who hasn't even been recognized as a man yet?" Cinthia asked.

"Well, that doesn't mean . . . what I am saying is," Royce stuttered. "But he still attacked me. What was I supposed to do, let him kill me?"

"Was it your place to correct the leader of a house, or do you think that was something better left to the adults?" Cinthia said, setting down the cream and directing her full attention to Royce.

"I believe that if someone attacks a royal official, especially in the royal courts, especially when that person is not another royal official, the penalty is death. If a civilized country such as yours has those laws, what do you think should happen to you in this martial culture for attacking the wife of Yao?"

Royce slowly lowered himself onto a seat as Cinthia's words sunk in.

"You are not a slave here, but every member of our culture must contribute to the needs of the tribe. There are no free rides, no exceptions. And as you are not a trained fighter, your place is here," Cinthia said, rising. "And one more thing. We call you Roe to protect you and us, not as an insult. If people learned that there was a Royce on this island and he appeared around the time that a Royce disappeared from the Island of the Mighty . . ." And with that, Cinthia left the kitchen.

Royce sat there for several minutes before returning to his feet and making his way to the wood pile. Picking up the axe, he began chopping firewood with a new determination.

* * *

Later that evening, he had found himself a sturdy branch and, after trimming it down, began mimicking the other fighters' sword moves.

"Well, look at this," June said, walking up with the other raiding party members. "You think you can just wave a stick around, and maybe we will take you in as a warrior? If you ask me, Yao should have left you back among the Sardinians because you don't belong here. You people from the big island come here and think we have to grovel for whatever job you want us to do."

Royce tried to walk away, but his path was blocked. Raising his stick brought laughs from the other Yaoites. June drew his sword and held its blade towards Royce.

"If you think you have what it takes to beat me with a wooden sword, come on."

"If you call yourselves Yaoites, why are you such a bad fighter? I saw Yao fight dozens of the islanders, and he didn't use a sword. What's your problem?" Royce taunted.

"That's a fair point," June said, placing his sword back in its sheath. "Take your best shot."

Royce swung with all his might at the older kid's head, and without even flinching, June stopped his wooden sword with his bare hand, just inches from his head. He proceeded to take it from him and beat him with it.

"Go back home, big island boy," June said, leaving Roe lying panting and bleeding on the ground. "You don't belong here."

Chapter 6

Roe was waiting on Wuji the following day and already had the oven fire roaring and the water pots filled.

"If it's all right with you, I would like to bring Yao his breakfast today."

"Well, I suppose it couldn't hurt anything. Except he is currently away helping some lord or another with some skirmish, from what I hear. One thing to remember when serving him breakfast is that he likes his morning meal served in absolute silence. Even Cinthia—"

A defining boom was followed by a rushing torrent of wind as the sky darkened.

"I thought we would have more time," Wuji yelled. "Strap the cart to the runner beast, and don't waste time doing it!"

Roe could barely distinguish what the old cook was saying as the winds and thunder turned their island into chaos. He aided Wuji in carrying a few items to the cart before attempting to fasten it to the frightened beast.

"Careful of those two legs," Wuji screamed as he leaned over to Roe. "I have seen those runner beasts stomp the life out of a full-grown warrior before when frightened."

As the two wrestled the harness through the straps already in place, the runner beast frantically struggled against the wind in the direction Wuji steered him. It took them over an hour to reach their destination, even though it was just off the beach. Once inside the caves, the runner beast hurried to the back as the rest of the warriors struggled through the entrance. Wet and exhausted, Roe leaned against the cool cave wall.

"Up, up, hurry! The best part is about to come! You definitely don't want to miss it," Wuji said as he and the others climbed to the lookout holes in the higher parts of the cave. Upon joining the old man, Roe strained to see through the storm and debris. He watched as roofs, fences, and even huts were picked up and tossed into the sea among blinding flashes of lightning.

"It's called a Galeforce, and they whip up out of nowhere and usually last all day. You picked a good season to come and stay with us but just wait," Wuji said.

Moments later, one of the Yaoite women screamed and began pointing and jumping up and down as others slowly began to cheer and clap. Roe strained to see what they were so excited about as their cheering and applause competed with the storm outside. Then his entire world changed.

He could barely make out green flashes of lightning and something moving in the storm some distance out at sea. Above the wind, a horn sounded, resulting in more tremendous elation from the Yaoites. Then it happened. The waters seemed to part and what could only be described as a glowing golden ringed serpent rose into the air. The serpent seemed to defy all the laws of gravity as it slithered through the air without the aid of wings. Royce realized that the horn sound he had heard earlier emanated from the serpent.

As if the Galeforce wasn't enough, the creature's bellows vibrated Royce's very core as it drew nearer. Flashes of green lightning surrounded it as it twisted and turned on the wind. The closer it got, Royce realized that it was easily twice the size of their entire island. The serpent and the storm seemed locked in combat for dominance. A dark funnel illuminated by momentary flashes of brilliance twisted its way across the water. The green light of the serpent circled the funnel as it rose into the heavens. All that could be seen through the torrent were flashes of green as the bellows caused even the rocks around them to shudder.

Turning away from a blinding flash, Royce noticed someone outside the cave, pinned against an outcropping of rock by the wind. He attempted to get Wuji's attention, but the old man, along with the others, were enraptured by the spectacle in the heavens. Climbing back through the cave, he found a sturdy rope and fastened one end to his waist. The other he secured as best he could around one of the stalagmites before wading out into the storm.

The wind and harsh, cold rain sucked the air out of his lungs, and within seconds he was dangling at the end of his rope between heaven and earth. As he dangled helplessly, a slight lull in ferocity dropped him into the slick sand. Straining to where he last saw the person, he crawled against the wind to the rocks and managed to find the unconscious body of a woman.

He struggled to tie a section of the rope around her ankle to keep her from being carried out to sea. The only thing Royce could do was huddle against the rock as he held on to the rope with all his might. A bellowing out at sea drew his attention as the serpent breathed fire at the twisting water funnel. As it raged against nature, brilliant gold and red tongues of flame swirled around each other, connecting the dark, choppy waves with the boiling heavens in a plume of light. Royce sat mesmerized as the people above him gave a thunderous cheer.

The serpent turned away from the fire funnel and headed directly towards the island. He wove along the leaping waves, coming to a dead stop in the middle of the air. Suddenly the storm around Royce lessened. Royce could only stare as the massive golden bands expanded and contracted. Was the serpent purposefully blocking the wind? Without waiting for an invitation, Royce dragged the Lady into the cave. Seconds later, the serpent departed to go play with nature.

Royce untied the rope from the Lady and gasped as Cinthia regained consciousness. She regarded him as he helped her to her feet, realizing what had just happened. She weakly thanked him with a smile after the island had somewhat recovered from the damage of the Galeforce. Royce began his training as a Yaoite warrior.

Chapter 7

It had been five grueling years since Royce, who had severed his identity and truly become Roe, had saved Cinthia's life, but no matter how hard he trained, Yao simply ignored him. He had mastered the bow and had gone up against some of the most seasoned warriors on a runner beast. As he rode, he had shot ten of the ten birds he had targeted both on land and in the water but there was not so much as a single word of acknowledgment, let alone praise, from Yao.

After a particularly hard day of riding and hunting, Roe had just finished brushing and feeding his mount when he saw a boat land on the beach and an armed invader, covered from head to foot in black, emerge. He watched as the invader made his way towards the jungle's shadows while keeping a low profile. He knew the other Yaoites were halfway through their meal by now, so he grabbed his short sword and set out in pursuit.

The invader darted behind a shed. Roe drew his sword and waited before the building for him to emerge. Moments later, the darkly clad man crept past him and headed toward the other huts.

"Stop right there and drop your weapons," Roe challenged.

The invader spun and drew his sword. The blade was curved, but before Roe could get a good look at it, the invader threw two darts in his direction. Easily swatting them aside, he charged the invader while lunging with his sword. The man moved like a leaf driven by the wind. He spun to avoid the attack and smashed the pommel of his sword into the base of Roe's skull as he passed.

Lights exploded in his vision as he closed his eyes, focusing all his efforts on his hearing, but the man had stopped moving. As the throbbing at the base of his skull lessoned, he opened his eyes to see the man watching him. Roe gradually circled to place himself between him and the village. Advancing, he kept the tip of his blade lowered and off to his right side. Suddenly lunging, he swung it up to meet the invader's downward slice and, moving with the impact, reversed the direction of his attack, bringing his sword on top of the other with all his might. The strike knocked the curved blade to the ground.

Raising the tip to the invader's throat, he was surprised as he swatted it aside with one hand while grabbing the handle and wrestling it free with the other. Tossing the sword aside, the invader removed his mask to the applause of the other Yaoites who had silently gathered to watch Roe and Yao spar.

"You didn't hesitate to defend your home despite your fatigue. You pushed through your injuries and didn't rely on others to save you. As Yao of this tribe, it is my decision that you are ready to serve in the smallest capacity on one of my raiding parties. Prepare yourself; tomorrow night is the night of the full moon. It is there that you will fulfill your duty to this island and take your place as a Yaoite."

In all the time Roe had spent on the island, he had never seen an initiation ceremony. When the following evening came, the island was dark as Roe stood on the walkway between the huts, wearing nothing but a loincloth. As the moon reached its full zenith, a powerful voice boomed from the semi-darkness.

"Step forward, Roe. Yao commands this."

As he began walking towards the voice, there was a whoosh as warriors on either side of him ignited the substance on their blades and held them up in salute. One by one, the path was illuminated for him until he came directly before Yao. Upon his arrival, the warriors formed a circle around him and lowered the tips of their blades to the ground. Yao stepped forward, holding an outfit of deep ocean blue, and addressed Roe.

"You had nothing when you came, and it was *my* job to give you food, it was *my* job to train you, it was *my* job to clothe you and to arm you. Your needs are *mine* to meet. As for you, you have but one duty, to lay down your life for Yao. If this pleases the clan, WHAT SAY YOU ALL!?"

"Yaoite, Yaoite, Yaoite," came the reply.

"You entered this night naked and alone, but let the dawn find you born into our family."

Later that night, Wuji and Cinthia brought out platter after platter of foods Roe had never seen before, and to his surprise, Yao served all of his warriors before eating himself. He laughed for the first time in years and enjoyed the banquet prepared in his honor.

Leaning back on his cushion, he gazed up at the stars and allowed himself to breathe the night air in deeply. As he watched the twinkling lights above, some of them began to fall through the heavens. Roe had seen many shooting stars, but there was something different about these. They grew closer and closer until the flaming arrows descended on the festival. With a scream, Sardinian warriors lept from their hiding place and attacked the banquet. Roe grabbed his sword as something smashed into his head, and everything went black.

With the rising of the sun, Roe and the few remaining Yaoites surveyed the damage. Most of the huts were little more than burnt shells, and dead bodies of the Yaoites and Sardinians littered the ground. Roe noticed June was sitting on the ground holding a garment, and . . . was it possible? Was June actually crying?

"Yaoites!"

Yao stood, bleeding and bruised, among numerous bodies of fallen Sardinian warriors.

"Prepare yourselves. They came and attacked us during our celebration and took our people. They think we will not pursue them lest harm comes to them, but I assure you, Cinthia and Wuji are not afraid to die."

CHAPTER 8

As a foreign galleon made its way towards the island of the Yaoites, the warriors prepared to rescue their tribesmen. The average galleon was used to transport troops. Under normal circumstances, each held 200 soldiers along with a captain and crew.

"Yao, won't the fighters on Sardinians Island be prepared for us?" Roe asked as he secured a bag of firebrands.

"You can be assured that they are well prepared for us."

"So, what's our plan? Don't they already outnumber us five to one?"

"Our plan?" Yao said, stretching his weary muscles. It was clear that he hadn't slept in the past thirty-six hours.

"Our plan is to get our people back," he said, tossing a bag full of arrows into the nearest boat.

The galleon lowered three longboats into the water. Each boat had a row of shields on either side. Judging from the shield count, that was only about half of their crew, assuming the galleon was alone, which was rarely the case.

"Will we be splitting up and attacking them from two different directions, and while they are engaged, will we send a third party to rescue our people?" Roe offered.

"Nope, we won't divide up our forces any further. We will stay together and attack them all at once."

Galleons were the sole property of the royal courts and, as such, contained the most seasoned soldiers in any kingdom. In fact, before even being considered for the royal army or navy, you had to have proven yourself in service to one of the five houses of the Island of the Mighty.

"Will we wait for nightfall, then attack?" Roe asked, eyeing the approaching longboats.

"No, we won't allow our people to wait longer than necessary in enemy hands. That's not our way. You remember how soon you were rescued when you were imprisoned?"

As the first of the longboats made landfall, the soldiers disembarked and stood at the ready for a fight. Only then did Roe realize that these were no ordinary soldiers; they were the capital's elite. Each man was expected to kill at least ten men in combat.

"Forgive me, Yao, but I believe my training hasn't prepared me for this. I have only received individual assassin fighting skills and know nothing of organized military tactics."

Yao studied his newest warrior for a minute. Roe couldn't be sure whether it was weariness or disappointment he saw in his eyes. "You'll be fine," he said before walking off towards the warriors who had just landed on his island. Roe hesitated only a moment before joining him.

As Yao approached the first sentry, he held up his hand for Yao to wait. Yao left him face down and unconscious in the sand. The next warrior leveled his spear at him, which Yao grabbed directly below the blade and, with one swift chop, broke the staff and ran the blade through the soldier's neck. The other soldiers leveled their spears at him before a command came for them to stop. A thin, pale-looking man in clothes that were a size too big for him stepped out of the second boat with much effort. It was clear that the voyage hadn't been kind to him.

"Forgive me, Lord Yao, is it?"

"It's just Yao."

"Er, Yao then. Please forgive my men and me. I have been sent here on the most urgent—"

"I don't know you. Strangers aren't welcome here. Get off of my island before you anger me."

Roe recognized Chancellor Ephron, but this was the first time he had seen him outside the royal courts.

"I apologize and have no intention of angering you. Begging your forgiveness, but I am under strict orders from Regent Sovans to contact you regarding a direst—"

"Ivan, I know. You, I don't. Leave," Yao said, turning his back on the official.

"Regent Ivan sent me here because the High King is dead."

As Yao froze, the world began to spin around Roe. *FATHER!*

Turning, Yao waited for the chancellor to approach before continuing.

"As you may know, the Contest of Kings is held every five years on the island of the Mighty, and last year, the title of 'sovereign' was again awarded to Sovereign Leotan. Last week the sovereign was found dead in his chambers, and Regent Ivan has ascended in his place until another Contest of Kings can be held and the new sovereign determined.

"Regent Ivan strongly suspects that the sovereign's death was at the hands of the assassin Lefterry. He has sent me to commission you to find and apprehend this assassin by any and all means necessary."

"You need a fully armed galley to deliver this message?" Yao asked, steadily gazing at the chancellor.

"Yes, er, well, you see, you have a reputation, and as this is my first time encountering you . . ."

Yao stood motionless, staring out at the waves for several long minutes. Before turning away and heading back to his men, he uttered a single word: "No."

Roe sat down heavily among the sand and surf. Why wasn't he happy at the news? Why wasn't he sad? It had been five years since he arrived on this island, and there had yet to be a messenger or a letter from home. Maybe he could accept this of his father with the duties and responsibilities of the realm, but indeed his mother would have tried or Uncle Ivan. Over the past five years, he had come to accept that his own family didn't want him, that he was dead to them, so why did it matter now when he had finally been accepted by the Yaoites?

"Yao," he called feebly. Whether he had heard him or not, it wasn't clear. He just kept walking.

"Equip every boat with whitebait. We leave within the hour."

CHAPTER 9

As Roe paddled his hooded boat, he realized they had left their entire island defenseless with a foreign gallery of elite soldiers having made landfall. But what was there to defend? Some grass huts, a cave, and some secondary weapons. All of the primary weapons were with them.

Suddenly the waters around them began to churn and boil as visions of a serpent larger than their entire island crashed into Roe's mind.

"Restrain your hand with the whitebait and keep following my lead," Yao said.

Moments later, Roe felt something bump against the underside of his boat. He gripped the boat's sides and watched as Yao dove into the waters. Moments later, he surfaced on the back of a green-finned sea creature that rode at the head of a pack. The green gilded sea creatures leapt into the air and glided alongside the warriors' boats as they tossed them white bait.

As Sardinians Island drew closer, the creatures departed as Yao returned to his boat. Directing them to a tiny beach with pounding waves that reached over his head on either side of them, he motioned for them to hurry and follow. Well versed in the hand and arm signals, Roe understood that the tide was only momentarily low. He watched, then imitated the other warriors as they secured their boats and launched their hooks up the black cliff facing them.

His first attempt to snag his hook fell short, but with his third, he secured a stronghold. He was the last of the warriors to begin the ascent up the slick rock surface. Upon reaching the summit, Roe realized he was alone. He started crawling towards the nearest bushes, but just as he arrived in the shadows, he saw the back of a Yaoite warrior vanish into the forest.

"Haste leads to discovery,"' he had been repeatedly taught.

Slowly making his way through the forest towards the sound of people working and talking and an abundance of animals, he stumbled over June concealed under a tree. Instantly they had blades to each other's throats before recognition separated them. Roe bowed an apology as June hurried towards the village. Upon reaching the spot he had gone through, Roe gently peered through the thicket and couldn't see him or any of the Yaoites.

A pebble bounced off his head, and he turned to see June motioning him back into the forest. Roe followed him until they reached a clearing with a large building in it. Guards patrolled the roof; directly below them, Yao used hand and arm signals to organize his raiders.

It was my job to give you food, it was my job to train you, it was my job to clothe you and to arm you. Your needs are mine to meet. Yao was the embodiment of what a true Sovereign should be, Roe thought.

Roe crept through the open side door, past the dead guards, and saw June disappear around a corner. Glancing through the bars of a locked cell, there was something familiar about the prisoner huddled in the dark corner of the room. Breaking open the door, he slowly crept towards the prisoner, his sword raised in defense. A familiar moan brought Roe to the side of his oldest friend and the best cook on the island.

Motioning for Wuji to stay close, Roe looked down the corridor he would be turning his back towards. A stream of guards headed in the direction June had gone. Motioning for Wuji to head toward the exit, Roe headed in the direction the guards came from and secured the doorway using the weapons of fallen guards.

He caught up to the end of the guards and began to silently drop them one by one. As he approached the room June was in, a peek around the corner revealed him holding an unconscious Cinthia as he wiped the blood from her face. Three guards were making their way toward him while trying to remain undetected. The nearest guard brought the butt of his spear down causing June to crumple to the floor.

Roe dispatched the closest guard before being attacked by the other two. Each of them had over a hundred pounds on him, and from what he knew, they had been fighting longer than he had been alive. He dodged the nearest attack using his size and speed before thrusting his sword through the guard's shoulder. Turning, he blocked the downward slash of the last guard with his blade while struggling to stay upright. As the wounded guard charged, Roe spun and allowed the previous guard's sword to slice the charging guard.

With the wounded guard incapacitated, Roe traded blows with the remaining guard until reducing him to a quivering pile of bloody meat. Turning towards the door, Roe held Yao's gaze before the Yaoite leader departed to ensure their escape.

* * *

Back on Yaoite Island, Roe tended to Wuji's wounds as the old man fussed at him for making a fuss.

"Roe, Yao has summoned you," a dejected June said, entering the kitchen.

As Roe approached the great hall a few steps ahead of June, Cinthia glanced his way before departing. Upon entering, Roe quickly realized that only the generals, captains, and raid leaders were present.

"Roe, you will stand before all gathered," Yao commanded.

As Roe did as he was told, Yao faced his commanders.

"It is on the field of battle that a man learns of his courage. Other arenas require men to be men, but in battle, where life and death are determined upon one's hesitation, our newest warrior has saved the life of a raid leader, and as such, I am raising him to the position of raid leader."

CHAPTER 10

“ I have spoken with Yao, and he agrees with me," June said. "As young as you are, you could benefit from an experienced leader like myself. From this moment on, I will personally critique your every thought, motive, and decision. Because unless you still haven't learned, you don't belong here. You aren't one of us, and you will never be."

Just as Roe decided it would not be the best time to test June's sense of awareness with flying sharp, pointy objects, the sun turned a dull brown, and a horizontal tear appeared in the fabric of space above the beach that opened like an eye. Radiant light spilled through the tear, and Roe was looking into an image of another land. Moments later, an elderly lady with dark brown leathery skin appeared, accompanied by two others. Leaning on her crooked staff, her blue eyes seemed to pierce Roe's soul.

"Warriors of Yao Island, I am Vivian, Magistrate of the Zuzax tribe. We request your aid. Since the death of Sovereign Leotan, marauders have invaded our land, and we are being overrun. We wish you to discover who is employing these marauders and convince them to never attack us again. Please hurry; our numbers are dwindling by the day."

With that, the tear mended itself, and the sun returned to its usual brilliance. Roe hurried to the great hall along with the other leaders. Approaching the door at the same time as June, he was shoved aside as June entered. The hall was already packed, and

Roe quickly learned the vision had appeared all across their island, wherever people were gathered.

"—just got back from Sardinians Island, and our forces are depleted. Would it be wise to stretch ourselves out any further at this time? And as the Sardinians aren't known for letting things go, can we afford to send our forces away if they could attack at any minute?"

Roe recognized the speaker as General Trazu, one of Yao's oldest commanders. Sliding into a seat along the back of the room, he waited the customary time until he would be allowed to speak. As Trazu took his seat, Captain Ninus rose.

"Let us not forget that farming and fishing are not how we make our living. We have already done damage to our reputation with the Sovans, who are our strongest allies. What damage would turning down this request cause?"

As Ninus took his seat, the hall fell into a murmur of conversations. Yao sat silently, waiting for his commanders to present their opinions, starting with the most senior down to the least experienced.

"I don't think we even need to consider answering this Vivian lady," June said. "She didn't even tell us where she lived. You would think that if she wanted us to take her seriously, she would at least tell us how to get to her."

"She comes from the Island of the Mighty," Roe said as others regarded him with scowls of disapproval. He hadn't technically spoken out of line. June was the second to youngest leader present, but there were several commanders between him and Captain Ninus.

"The Zuzax tribe are indigenous to the island, and most of the royal houses have forced them into servitude. Magistrate Vivian leads those who reside on the barren north side of our island. It is common for a house to require more servants to raid the northern lands."

"You need to wait until your betters have had their say before you open your mouth again," June said to cover his ignorance.

"Commanders," Cinthia said, rising from her seat beside Yao. "We must find a way to repair our defenses while fulfilling our obligations as warriors. The quickest way to mend our defenses is with the means we get from completing missions. The question before us now is what kind of commitment will be required of us to stop those employing the marauders."

"I have heard enough," Yao said, rising as Cinthia took her seat. "We will send a scouting party to the Island of the Mighty to learn the strengths and weaknesses of the marauders. This is not to be a combat mission, and as we have one here who is educated in the ways of that Island, Roe will lead that mission. He is to take along three others to meet with Magistrate Vivian and understand the situation fully. With this knowledge, we will plan for the mission to follow. Yao has spoken."

Roe quickly left the hall, hoping to avoid June. Heading towards the kitchen, he thought it would be best to get Wuji's advice on who he should choose to accompany him on his first mission. No sooner had he entered the kitchen than he came face to face with June.

"You see, even Yao doesn't think you belong with us. Do you think this mission is just about finding out about the marauders? He's allowing you to return to your people. But don't worry, I will deliver the information Yao has requested. And as for the other party members, I have already selected them."

"Be careful of that one," Wuji said as Roe watched June leave.

"Any warrior who abandons his duties, especially in the middle of a mission, will be hunted down and killed. As you know, Yao places duty above all else."

CHAPTER 11

"We are here just to observe and report, nothing more because Yao knows you couldn't handle anything else," June said as the scouting party landed on the northeastern side of the Island of the Mighty.

"Yao also said that I am in charge, so we do things my way," Roe said, dragging his boat into the shrubs to conceal it.

"By all means, lead on. I am only here to tell Yao how badly you screw up."

After a few minutes of scouting along the beach, Roe discovered a footpath leading inland. A few hours later, they came upon a Zuzax village.

"June, you stay here. I will take one other warrior, and we will introduce ourselves to the magistrate. If we aren't back before sunset, something went wrong."

"Oh no. Where you go, I go. These two will stay here while we meet this woman," June said, starting without Roe.

As the two warriors entered the village, the people stopped their tasks and stared at them.

"Where is Vivian?" June loudly demanded.

"Shut your mouth before I break your teeth," Roe hissed, keeping his voice low.

Roe approached one of the oldest men, staring at him.

"Greetings, father," he said, giving a respectful bow. "I am Roe of the Yaoites. We come in answer to Lady Vivian's request. If it's convenient for you, please direct us towards the magistrate, and we will trouble you no further."

The old man's eyes widened slightly as he chuckled to himself.

"Yaoites, eh? You're a respectful one, but to these old eyes, you look like a Southerner."

The old man started to walk off, then stopped.

"You will find the Magistrate's house just north of the village," he said, laughing to himself as he continued on his way. "The Yaoites are now training Southerners; what's this world coming to?"

"You see? Even the Zuzax don't like you," June said to Roe's back as he headed in the direction the old man had indicated. Upon reaching the magistrate's home, they were met with the business end of two spears at the front door. After a brief explanation, they were relieved of their swords and escorted into a large room adorned with paintings of hunters and animals and a large castle that seemed centrally located in the middle of the island. Roe knew the castle was known as Valvatine from his childhood education, and journeying there was strictly forbidden. Arranged around the floor were several ornate cushions.

"Sit," the call came from outside of the room. Moments later, the Lady from the vision walked through the doorway directly across from where Roe and June stood. Roe bowed low while June stood erect, eyeing the old Lady with skepticism.

"I told you two to sit; why are you still standing? Is this the compliance the Yaoites exhibit to Yao on their island?" Magistrate Vivian said, seating herself on a bamboo chair.

"A thousand pardons, Magistrate Vivian. If we were to sit, how could we greet you with the respectful bow due to your personage?" Roe said, taking a seat in front and to the right of the magistrate. Moments later, June took a seat to the left.

"Well, your tone is respectful, but your appearance is offensive. What was Yao thinking about sending a Southerner to me? Does he have no sense?"

At this, June bristled, but Roe placed his hand on his arm.

"Again, a thousand pardons, your ladyship. My name is Roe, and we have arrived to ascertain the threat to your people. Once we understand this, we will proceed with the removal of the mercenaries from your lands."

"Did Yao not get my message? I want the heads, the people controlling the mercenaries, eliminated. What good does it do to kill one group? If you kill the head, the rest of the body follows."

"Yes, your ladyship, I beg your pardon. We are to discover the size of the threat and then inform Yao so he can determine the appropriate—"

"How old are you, boy?" Vivian asked, leaning forward in her chair.

"I am eighteen summers."

"What you are saying to me is that Yao doesn't take us seriously. He sends a boy and a Southerner, no less, to size up the marauders even though I never asked this of him. Tell me another party of adults is going to the marauder's base and clipping their head."

"Now you listen to me," June said, jumping to his feet. "We have just been invaded by the Sardinians, and we were in the process of rebuilding when your message came. It's not convenient for us to help you at this point, so why don't you just accept the help we offer and content yourself with that? If that doesn't work for you, find someone else to fight your battles for you."

Moments later, the two were escorted outside the magistrate's home.

"Let's go. We are wasting our time here. We should have never taken this mission while our people need us," June said, walking away from the house.

"June! You will respect the command of Yao. He was the one who placed me in charge here, and you will do well to remember that, or else I will report your activities to him."

June walked up to Roe until their noses were almost touching. Lowering his voice until it was nearly a whisper, he said, "That is the second time you have threatened me today. Do it again, and you won't make it back to Yaoite Island."

"Remain out here," Roe dauntlessly ordered.

As he made his way back inside, he prostrated himself before Vivian. Ignoring him for several minutes, she finally replied, "What do you want?"

"Magistrate Vivian, please understand that Yao does take your request seriously. We're recovering after our women and children were taken from us and our men slain. We were celebrating the ascension of a boy to a warrior. This cowardly attack has weakened us, but please, believe me, Yao is eager to meet your needs and alleviate your suffering."

"Well, I will not deny that I enjoy seeing a Southerner on his face before me. You people have enslaved and harassed my people by sending raiding parties into my territory for as long as I can remember."

"With respect, Magistrate Vivian, not all of the members of the Southern kingdom enslaved the Zuzax people. The House of Sovans has employed the services of the Zuzax people in direct opposition to every other house. Shouldn't the magistrate of the Zuzax nation take that into consideration?"

Vivian leaned forward and squinted at him. "Just who are you, boy?"

"My name is Royce Sovans, son of Leotan Sovans, Prince of the Five Realms. I come to you on behalf of the mighty Yao to aid you in your time of need."

Magistrate Vivian regarded him with her piercing blue eyes for several long moments. Finally, stirring herself, she stood. "If what you say is true, it doesn't matter. I still don't trust your kind."

And with that, she left the room.

CHAPTER 12

Roe sat there on his cushion, stunned. Not only had he revealed his identity, but he had also failed his first mission. As he reflected on this, a boy not more than a year younger than Roe entered the hall.

"You can't let Grammy Vivian get to you. She has a lot going on but needs all the help she can get. She tries to come across as tough, but she is a kind person. My name is Pomii; what's your name?"

"Roe."

Rising to leave, he was surprised to find Pomii standing in his way.

"I know a way that she has to accept you and work with you."

Roe stood still regarding the boy. He was about two inches shorter than him and a lot rounder. His dark brown skin and striking blue eyes beamed with a hope that Roe had all but forgotten.

"What are you talking about?"

"If we become brothers, Grammy will have to accept you," Pomii said with a smile.

* * *

The sun had settled hours ago as three Yaoites stood among a circle of Zuzax tribesmen. In the center, Roe and Pomii stood with their shirts off and a knife in their hands. Without a sound, they both carved a six-pointed star into their wrists. As the blood flowed, they grasped each other's forearms, overlying the cut star with the other.

Magistrate Vivian approached the two, also with a knife in her hand. She held it up to one of the long locks of her hair and sliced it off. Taking the strand, she tied it around the wrists of the two before her.

Without a sound, the two began to wrestle and pull against the strand. After what seemed like an eternity, the strand of hair finally broke. The two sat on the ground panting as Vivian bandaged their wounds.

"Tonight, you have become my blood brother, Roe of the Yaoites," Pomii said. This land belongs to you as much as it does to me. My blood flows through your veins as yours does mine. What's mine is yours and what's yours is mine."

* * *

The following evening, the Yaoite warriors set out with Pomii south toward the marauder's camp. While en route, they encountered the party. As the Yaoites proved their skills against the eight scouts, Pomii hid in the bushes.

"These are Dular mercenaries," Roe said, wiping the blood from his sword. "Their land is the farthest south of any of the five houses. They are too heavily armed just to be capturing slaves."

"Well, a lot of good these guys will do us," June said, removing his sword from one of the mercenaries. "It's not like they can tell us who their leader is when they are dead."

"Do these guys normally change clothes between camping and scouting?" Pomii asked upon emerging from his hiding spot and carefully stepping over the bodies.

"What do you mean?" Roe asked.

"I mean that these guys dress differently than the guys that crossed the River Wade," Pomii replied.

"That's because the other people are probably soldiers that came along to guard the prisoners, and these are mercenaries sent to capture you guys," June replied.

"Not necessarily," Roe said. "Dular soldiers and mercenaries dress alike. Pomii, could you take us to where the differently dressed people are?"

"We are going to need provisions. It's over two days' ride from here," Pomii said, heading back toward their village.

Later that night, Pomii sketched their semicircle route towards the River Wade from the Zuzax tribe.

"Why are you taking us the long way to the river?" June asked, glaring at Pomii. "If we cut through this Homini pass, it would be more of a direct route, and according to your map, the terrain is smoother."

"We can't go there; that route passes through the blue lands."

"What's a blue land?" Roe asked.

"You don't know what the blue lands are, brother? The blue lands are where Magi battled the invaders from the Land of Ever-Night a hundred years ago. The space between our realms is weakest in the blue lands, and creatures from there cross over here. If you journeyed there, you could slip into a land of eternal darkness and never come out."

* * *

The party set off at first light, and as they came up on the peak of a mountain to the east of the blue land, Pomii pointed to a sizeable six-legged animal in the distance that was eating the vegetation.

"Have you ever seen an animal that large and with six legs?" Pomii asked. "But that's only half of it. The other half is stuck in the blue lands. He has been that way for as long as I have been alive."

The party grew closer to the River Wade as night approached. Several fires could be seen on the beach as shadows moved around them. Urging Pomii to stay behind with the runner beasts, the scouting party crept to the foliage's edge and watched the invaders. Two large tents were erected among dozens of smaller ones. The Yaoites watched as two men wearing different uniforms approached the edge of their encampment.

"Lieutenant Voltaire, any report from your marauders?" the older one asked.

"Nothing yet, Captain Monicum. If they haven't returned by morning, I will assume they have been lost to us and send out another party."

Captain Monicum was a seasoned Nominious veteran. Even though his hair was greying around the edges, one look told anyone that he still had a good deal of fight in him.

"Just make sure they get back soon. The main party arrives in a few days, and I need to inform my commanders about the lay of the land."

When the wiry lieutenant hurried off, Roe raised two fingers and waved in the direction they came.

"Those were Nominious soldiers," Roe said. "If they are working with Dular mercenaries, this isn't a slave drive; this is an invasion!"

CHAPTER 13

"Mount up. The sooner we get back to Yaoite Island, the sooner we can report back to Yao," June said.

"And tell him what exactly? We still need to find out how many soldiers are coming and who the head of the marauders is. What if this comes from the Duke of Dular or the Noble of Nominious? Are you suggesting we kill the heads of two houses? If you thought the Sardinians were tough, what do you think fighting the entire standing army would be like?"

"Fine," June said, removing his pack from the runner beast. "But the longer we delay, the more danger we place the Zuzax people in."

"We will stay here until we learn how many soldiers are already here and how many are coming. Then we will be able to provide Yao with a complete report."

"How, exactly, are you planning on learning that? Maybe we could just ask them nicely?" Ignoring June, Roe began to make his way back to the beach. Upon arriving, they saw two bands of eight marauders assembled before Lieutenant Voltaire.

"The last group headed due north. This time the first squad will circle from the east, and the second squad will circle around from the west."

The Yaoites watched the Dulars disappear into the darkness as Voltaire made his way toward the largest tent on the beach. It bordered the river to the south and was surrounded by dozens of smaller tents. Motioning for the Yaoites to follow him, Roe circled the encampment and slid into the water. Swimming back towards the camp, they emerged and crept to the commander's tent. Hiding among the boats that lay alongside the tent, Roe looked across the river to the far shore where the twinkling lights of the Southern kingdom could be seen. He knew that they were directly north of the lands held by House Nominious.

". . . expected by this time tomorrow," Captain Monicum was saying. "When the second wave of soldiers arrives, we want to move out immediately. We will leave a platoon to hold this beach while the rest of the troops move toward the castle. If all goes according to plan, and we know that nothing ever does, the Nominious flag will fly in the Northern kingdom by next week."

June motioned for Roe to move back towards the water, but Roe motioned to stay. Disregarding this, June and the other two Yaoites moved away, leaving Roe behind. Deciding that he needed to stay with the group, he slowly followed them.

Arriving at their rendezvous point at the edge of the camp, where they had first encountered the lieutenant and captain, he found that he was alone. Looking around, he discovered that June was already making his way back to Pomii and their runner beasts.

"What was that!? You deliberately disobeyed me. We could have learned a lot more if we had stayed and listened," Roe said, preparing to draw his sword. June ignored him as he prepared for bed.

"That little swim of yours was a waste. I have all the information that I need," he finally replied. "We know numerous soldiers are coming and who is sending them. We have only so many fighters, and as you pointed out, we cannot take out the head of a house, so what are we still waiting around here for? This mission is a bust."

"When we get back, I am going to make sure Yao is fully informed of your usurpation of the authority of a raid leader," Roe said, still gripping his sword.

"Go ahead. Don't care," June replied, rolling away from Roe.

As the night darkened, Pomii brought out a clear globe suspended from cords and removed the lid. Producing an ocarina, he leaned against a tree and began to play softly. June rolled over and moved to stop him, but Roe intervened.

"What are you, some kind of stupid? He is going to give our location away," June hissed.

"Just listen," Roe replied.

Within moments, that tune was heard throughout the night as music danced across the Northern kingdom.

"You know nothing of Northern ways," Roe said. "When I was younger, my family used to go camping in the wilds. Every night we heard the Zuzax music, quelling the savage lands sometime after nightfall and before midnight. Don't worry; things should quiet down when you take the next watch."

As Pomii played, flying specks of light surrounded him. Waving his hand in a circular motion, he collected the specks and directed them into his globe, replacing the lid. Hanging the globe from a long branch, he placed the map under the light. With the globe hanging three feet off the ground, the glow didn't quite reach the tops of the shrubs. Roe and the other Yaoite lay on their stomachs and studied the map.

"Exactly where is the Northern castle anyway?" Roe asked Pomii. "I have always known there was one, but every time I met them, they always came to the South to ask for food and supplies."

Pomii indicated a section directly in the center of the Northern lands.

"Why is this section all blacked out?"

"Because that is where the cursed princess lives," Pomii replied.

"But that section is where the soldiers are heading. Do you have another map of that area?"

"No, no one does," Pomii said. "That land is forbidden to us."

"Who forbade you to go there?"

"Magistrate Vivian when she cursed the royal family."

"Why would she do such a thing? I thought the northern kingdom was friendly to the Zuzax people," Roe asked.

"That's a very long story, but one thing I can tell you right now is that if you plan on going there, you will have to go there without any help from the Zuzax people."

"We need to warn them of the coming army. It's only fair. I would like you to come with me, but I don't want you to do anything that gets you in trouble with Grammy."

"If you are determined to go there," Pomii replied, "then Grammy would be more upset with me if I abandoned my blood brother. Before you go, you need to learn the story of the cursed princess and why Grammy has forbidden any of us from going there."

Chapter 14

"Do you know how Emperor Elgin came to the northern kingdom?" Pomii asked.

"I was taught that he was once a merchant who had moved here from the Forest of Thebes. He gained wealth in trade with all of the five houses, but a dispute arose between his fleet and the fleet of House Kastlet. Count Christoff claimed that his merchant ships disrupted the fishing industry, where he made his fortune. He took it to the high courts, where King Dular was reigning.

"It wasn't much of a case," Roe continued. "The sovereign sided with one of the five houses against the foreigner. To side with an outsider against a ruling house would be considered treason. House Dular and House Nominious wanted to continue trade with Elgin at the expense of Count Christoff. Still, after the ruling, Elgin moved to the Northern wastelands and declared himself emperor."

"Huh, I never knew all that," Pomii said. "This all happened before I was born. I have been taught that after Emperor Elgin built his castle, he soon fell in love with Aunt Cleo. They were married, and everybody seemed happy. Elgin's kingdom grew, and he even placed guards around the island and told the Southern kingdom that if any of them came to the Northern lands to make slaves of our people, he would take that as an act of war."

"I remember being taught this in history class," Roe said. "Because a declaration of war is such a serious affair, it requires a unanimous vote by all five houses. The end count was four to one with House Sovans voting against the other houses."

"I didn't know about that either. All we knew was that the Southern kingdom left us alone, and things were good."

"Then what happened?" Roe asked.

"Lilith happened, that's what," Pomii shouted.

Looking around to see if his response had drawn any attention, Roe encouraged his brother to continue in a softer voice.

"With the announcement that Aunt Cleo was pregnant, everybody was happy until it came time for her to give birth. That was when your people started sending us criminals."

With a groan, Roe told of how House Belthane, which housed the prison colony, had made a secret deal with the Kastlets to use some of their boats. They then loaded up some of the worst criminals and exiled them to the port of Celestias in the Northern kingdom. They told them they would face a swift execution if they ever returned to the Southern kingdom. In all, three boats landed on the northernmost shore and deposited passengers there.

"All that started the night Lilith was born and Aunt Cleo died in childbirth," Pomii continued. "Emperor Elgin sent out the army to capture the criminals, but most of them would rather fight than be captured again, so many of our people, including my father, were killed. That was how it all began. With the death of aunt Cleo, Grammy's heart couldn't take anymore, so she put a curse on the castle and forbade our people from going there."

"Do you believe that stuff, though?" Roe asked. "Just because someone says that they cursed somebody else doesn't mean anything."

Pomii just shook his head and watched the flying specs of light dance around the orb.

"Have you ever been to the Castle Valvatine on Center Island?" he asked without looking up.

Located in the center of the River Wade was an island with a vast, abandoned castle. Nobody knew exactly where the castle came from or why it was abandoned. But everybody knew that the castle was older than anything else on the Island of the Mighty. Many rumors said that the Zuzax had ruled the land from that castle, and after an internal feud, the entire island split in half while the castle remained on its own island.

"Everybody knows of the Castle Valvatine," Roe said.

"Do you know why nobody lives there anymore? Because one of the ancient magistrates cursed it because of the blood shed there."

"How would you even prove something like that? Anybody can say they did this or that, but how can you directly prove that their actions are actually responsible for the outcome?" Roe said incredulously.

"I can't explain it to you," Pomii replied. "All I know is that since Grammy cursed Emperor Elgin, nothing has gone right for them. Several years later, a ship came from the emperor's people in the Forest of Thebes carrying his new wife. They were set to get married, but she died one night at the dinner table. They weren't just having dinner that night; they were also celebrating Lilith's birthday."

* * *

The Dular marauders slowly made their way to the east of their beachfront landing. They continued for hours until finally coming to rest among six unusual trees. When they dismounted, their runner beasts grew frantic, and one of them bolted off back towards the beach. After securing their mounts, the marauders realized that the six trees were actually six legs connected to an enormous animal.

"Get to the top of that ridge," their leader shouted.

Cresting the ledge with nothing but the stars to guide them, they made out an enormous animal protruding out of an invisible wall. Summoning one of the marauders, their leader instructed him to hurry back to camp and give them a complete description of what they had found to Lieutenant Voltaire. About a mile before he reached the beach, the scout heard voices from a cluster of trees. Dismounting, he crept up to the cluster and discovered four warriors and a Zuzax boy huddled between them. Moments later, he rode into camp and went directly to the commander's tent.

Upon waking Lieutenant Voltaire, the scout hurriedly told him everything they had encountered, ending with the camp of spies on their outskirts.

"This campaign is at a critical juncture. We need more than a beachfront holding, and with the main assault arriving soon, we need every inch of ground available. Wake one of the Nominious squad commanders and bring those spies to me. If they resist, kill them."

CHAPTER 15

Roe woke to the sound of a soft thump beside his head and, upon opening his eyes, discovered a dismembered hand still clutching a sword. Jumping to his feet along with the other Yaoites, he watched as June severed the head from an attacker's shoulders before moving on to the next. He figured it was about two in the morning when most people would be sound asleep. They had chosen their time to attack wisely but failed to account for June on night watch.

No sooner had he drawn his sword than five spear tips confronted him. Battling through them, he slew the soldiers and turned to aid the other Yaoites. Moments later, they looked around at about twenty bodies lying around their campsite.

"Pomii!" Roe called out.

A muffled cry was heard to the south of their camp, but as Roe started in that direction, June blocked his path.

"It's obviously a trap, you idiot."

"When you start caring about who Yao has placed in charge here, then you will be in a position to tell me what I can and cannot do. Until then, get out of my way."

Charging past June and into the darkness, he could barely make out a group of soldiers dragging a struggling prisoner away from their camp. He quickly covered the distance between them and dispatched the soldiers, freeing Pomii. No sooner had he released his brother than a look of horror came over Pomii's face as the tip of a spear protruded from Roe's chest. The soldier holding the other end forced him to the ground. Moments later, the spear was yanked out of his body. He turned to see that June had dispatched the soldier.

"Wouldn't do to have you die on your very first mission, especially when I'm your—"

"JUNE!" Roe called as a Dular mercenary sword cleaved his head. Roe struggled to regain his feet, but he was quickly knocked down as more mercenaries surrounded him. As he slowly lost consciousness, the last thing he saw was June's lifeless eyes staring at him.

* * *

The rising sun's light stabbed Roe's eyes, and a heavy hand slapped him again.

"There you are, now tell me, where is the campsite for the rest of you killers?"

"June," he feebly managed to moan, earning him another slap.

"No, no. Let's try another question. What's your name?"

Roe saw that the other two Yaoites were receiving similar treatment, but he knew they would willingly die before talking. Attempting to breathe brought a sharp pain, and looking down, he saw a crude dressing around his abdomen.

"You know, you don't look like these other Yaoites, and you sure aren't a Northerner. Where are you from, boy?" asked Captain Monicum, but his further inquiries were also met with silence.

"I get it; you Yaoites are trained to withstand all kinds of questioning, but lucky for us, you weren't the only ones we captured."

Roe watched helplessly as Pomii's beaten body was dragged in front of him. At first, he could resist the questioning methods of the Nominious soldiers, but eventually, his untrained mind broke. Minutes later, Captain Monicum returned, and Roe was yanked to his feet.

"I like your brother there. Pomii turned out to be a wealth of information. Once you have a feel for the size of the invaders, you plan on reporting back to Yaoite Island. Well, it's a good thing for us that you will never make that trip, but I still have some questions that Pomii didn't know. How many Yaoites can we expect when you don't check in?"

While Roe continued to glare at the captain in silence, the captain appeared to relent.

"All right, you win. We are just going to send you to Nominious to get the answers. We have people there who specialize in that kind of thing."

While preparations were made for the journey south, Roe saw a couple of soldiers pass by with shovels. From their conversation, he learned that they had buried June. Two boats were made ready, and he and Pomii were roughly tied down at opposite ends of one while the two Yaoites were tied the same way in the other. As the Southern shore drew close, a flood of memories of home came with it.

It had been five years since he had been there. What had changed, and what had remained the same? Hours later, the boat docked, and any thoughts of escaping quickly vanished as they were handed over to the guards, and their ropes were replaced with iron bands.

"I'll bet he's from Belthane," the jailer said to one of the guards after looking at Roe. "Way I see it, he came from over there because our lands are the only two connected to the River Wade."

"Ya think so?" the guard replied. "I heard the Belthanes hated the Northerners because of that whole cursed princess thing."

"There's one way to find out," the jailer said. "Who do we know in Belthane who knows everybody? Let's get them over here and see if they can tell us just what region this guy comes from."

While Roe knew that anyone from Belthane would fail to recognize him, it was entirely possible that they would recognize him as belonging to the Sovans kingdom directly to their south.

"Meanwhile, let's get the questioner over here to pry some answers from these guys."

It took a second of looking around his cell for Roe to recognize Pomii. Shuffling over to his brother, he was relieved to see his chest rise and fall. Deciding to let him sleep for what was coming next, Roe looked down at the dark blood flowing from his injury. While he knew he could withstand the light questioning he had received in the Northern kingdom, a trained interrogator was a different matter entirely. It was only a matter of time before they discovered he was from Sovans. No matter how hard he resisted, the truth would eventually come out about who he was. He shuddered to think what they would do when they learned that they were holding the very person who was responsible for the Noble of Nominious's death five years ago.

CHAPTER 16

Pomii slowly sat up with a moan. Looking over at Roe, he tried to smile but soon changed his mind. Indicating the pool of blood Roe was sitting in, he asked how he was doing.

"I don't expect to die today, but I feel like it," he said between painful gasps.

Trying to keep his mind off what would happen, he urged Pomii to tell him more about the cursed princess.

"Why do the Belthanes hate the Northerners so much?"

"You mean you don't know the story?" Pomii asked.

"I have been training with the Yaoites for the past five years," Roe said as he tested the limits of his chains. One end was fastened to the wall while the other was firmly clamped to his ankle. He twisted the chain around in one direction as much as his wound would allow and then reversed the movement and twisted it in the other direction as hard as he could.

"It all started with the wedding announcement of Princess Lilith to Prince Belthane. We watched as ship after ship arrived and the merchants brought their wares. Emperor Elgin came from a very wealthy family of merchants, but he was the first of them to settle down and build a kingdom. Numerous exotic creatures had been imported from the Forest of Thebes. I remember this one that had eight legs but no feet or claws. It loved to climb on things, and I guess it was some kind of a healer.

"We would watch people lay down on a table with their shirts off, and this creature would walk on their back and knead their muscles the way my mom used to knead bread dough. Then it would pull and twist them very gently, and we would always hear their spines pop then snap back into place, and the people would sigh happily."

"I think you are describing an octovolt. They can generate a minimal amount of lightning, which helps if you have any muscle injuries. My dad had one, but I have never experienced their healing touch," Roe said as he twisted the chain the other way again.

"Then everybody started coming up from House Belthane, bringing foods we had never seen before."

"The lands belonging to House Belthane are known for their prisons and gardens. They produce almost all of the fruits and vegetables for the entire kingdom. The Sovans, just to the south of their lands, are known as masters of tradecraft. That and their runner beasts are the strongest and fastest on the island. To their west is House Dular, which has some of the finest artists in the entire kingdom. Everything from music to food to works of art. To the east of them, the small kingdom of Kastlet has the largest fishing fleet of any house. To the north of Kastlet, where we are, House Nominious raises cattle," Roe said between painful breaths.

"It was more than we had ever seen before," Pomii continued. "Then came the fateful wedding day. Emperor Elgin had ensured that the day was as far from Lilith's birthday as it could be, exactly six months. We watched everyone gather outside of the castle and then—"

"All right, you two, the moment you have been waiting for is here," the jailer said, opening their cell door. Accompanying him were two men, one who wore a smock covered in blood, and the other had the appearance of a Belthane. As the latter looked over Roe, he scoffed at the twisted chain holding him.

"That's not one of ours, but unless I miss my guess, he's Sovans. From what I hear, the Sovans have a contract with the Yaoites. You should have known that based on his clothes before you wasted my time dragging me down to your dungeon," the Belthane said as he departed.

The second man studied Pomii and Roe for a minute, then pointed to Pomii.

"Let's start with that one. The Sovans doesn't look like he would last more than a minute."

For the next several hours, the dungeon echoed with Pomii's screams as darkness descended on the dungeon. With the sound of somebody being dragged along the hallway, Roe immediately suspended his efforts on the chain. Moments later, Pomii was tossed back into the cell and shackled.

"'Bout time for my dinner," the questioner said. "You two make sure to get a good night's sleep so we can start fresh and early in the morning."

Moving his way over to Pomii, Roe did what little he could to treat his friend's wounds.

"I can't do that again," Pomii sobbed. "I would rather die before going through that."

"The trick is to think about something, anything else. Put your mind in another place, distract yourself from what's happening in the here and now."

"I don't know how to do that. How can you think of something else while they are cutting pieces off of your flesh?"

"You are in a great deal of pain. Finish telling me the story of the cursed princess," Roe said.

"I really don't want to do that right now."

"Now is when you must do it. Think. Remember. Take your mind off your present pain and tell me the story."

"Alright," Pomii said, trying to shift into a more comfortable position. "I guess we have until morning anyway."

Roe didn't have the heart to tell him that the questioner was trying to lull them into a false sense of security, and as soon as they fell asleep, they would be awakened to endure more torment.

"When the wedding day came, I snuck into the throne room and waited. Princess Lilith was also waiting at the back of the room along with Emperor Elgin, but Prince Belthane was not at the head of the room as he was supposed to be. Someone was sent to check in on him, and minutes later, they came back and announced that they'd found him dead in his room. We never learned the cause of death."

"HA!" Roe shouted as the weakest link in his chain broke away. Picking up the twisted piece of metal, he viciously rubbed it against the iron bars until a point began to form.

"Then what happened?" he asked after sitting back down to catch his breath while holding a hand over his wound.

"They called the whole thing off. Some people began blaming and harassing our people because of Grammy's curse, but Emperor Elgin put a stop to that. He really was good to our people," Pomii finished.

"What happened to the emperor?" Roe asked, resuming his work on the metal. Pomii just shook his head as he watched Roe.

"He died. Exactly one year to the day that his daughter's wedding was supposed to take place, his servants found him murdered in his bedroom."

"Who do they think did it?" Roe asked, sliding the sharp piece of metal into the lock holding his broken restraint. Seconds later, he was rewarded with a click as his cuff was released. Moving over to Pomii, he repeated the process. As the two of them hurried to the dungeon door, Roe looked expectantly at Pomii.

"We never found out who exactly killed him, but I kept hearing one name over and over: Lefterry."

Roe froze with the chain link still in the lock. Voices could now be heard coming toward their cell.

Shaking off all the questions that raced through his mind, he frantically worked the lock and was rewarded with a click of freedom as the jailer and questioner appeared at the other end of the hallway.

Chapter 17

“Quick, which way to the questioner’s chambers,” Roe whispered as they left their cell and slid along the wall.

“What!?” Pomii asked with a look of terror in his eyes.

“Which way?” Roe repeated, grabbing his friend by the shoulders.

Without responding, Pomii headed further into the dungeon. Just as they rounded a corner, a cry of alarm sounded. Pomii led them further down, and after several more turns, he brought them to a heavy door. Finding it unlocked and empty, the two armed themselves with the questioner’s instruments and hid. Several minutes later, they watched as the questioner preceded the two guards dragging an unconscious Yaoite warrior between them.

After fastening him into the restraints, the two guards left to join the search for Roe and Pomii. The questioner splashed dirty water onto the Yaoite and asked him his name. Without an answer, he picked up a small knife and cut away his shirt. Hearing a noise behind him, he turned and came face to face with Pomii holding one of his heavier instruments. The questioner brought up his knife as Pomii flew in a rage at him, knocking him to the floor as Roe freed the Yaoite.

“Now, now, I was just doing my job, nothing personal,” he stammered as he tried to crawl away.

Pomii raised and lowered his makeshift club several times until the questioner stopped moving.

"For the record, this wasn't me doing my job," he said, looking at the dead questioner. "This was personal."

"Do you know where they are keeping the other Yaoite?" Roe asked.

The Yaoite nodded, faithfully honoring the code of silence while on a mission. After arming himself, they headed out of the dungeon. Upon reaching the cell, Roe worked the locks and freed the remaining Yaoite. Then they made their way towards the outer door. While Roe opened the locks, the others kept watch for the guards. Moments later, two guards were heard walking past. Bursting through the door, the Yaoites quickly subdued the guards and clothed themselves in their armor.

"We came from that direction," Roe motioned.

As the group made their way toward the waterfront, they watched patrols of guards circling the grounds searching for them. Roe indicated they should grab two lanterns even though both moons were out in full force tonight. Lighting their lanterns, the group made their way toward the boatyard.

Upon arrival, they caught the attention of a carpenter working late.

"What's going on out there?"

"Manhunt," Roe called, nearly passing out with the effort.

"Manhunt, huh?" the carpenter said, making his way toward the group.

"You haven't seen anybody around here, have you?" Roe asked, keeping the light in the carpenter's eyes.

"Can't say I have. With the soldiers down by the water preparing to leave, they would be a darn fool to come this way. Besides, I ain't got no more boats," he said as he stepped in close. "Just who is it that escaped?"

Noticing Pomii and Roe's injuries, he looked up in terror at the Yaoites clothed in armor.

"Wait a minute; you aren't Nominious guards!"

Seconds later, he was unconscious and tied up in his workshop.

"Looks like he was right about there not being any boats around," Pomii said. An inspection of the dry docks revealed a boat that had been brought in for repairs.

"Beggars can't be choosers, I guess," Roe said as the Yaoites turned the wheels that raised the gate and allowed the sea into the dry docks. Minutes later, their boat floated in the water but leaned heavily to one side. The group climbed in and scrambled over to the high side. The two Yaoites worked the oars, but as the boat had just passed the dry dock gates, a shout was heard from the shore. They watched as the freed carpenter pointed at them while a group of guards formed on the coast.

The carpenter said something to the guards, causing them to laugh and turn away. As the water began to fill the boat, it became clear what they were laughing about. Roe squinted for the distant shores and could barely make out a rock formation. The Yaoites broke off pieces of timber, and as the group floated in the direction of the rocks, their boat sank. The Yaoites kicked and swam with all their might, not to be pulled under with suction, and finally managing to break free, they were hurled up against the rock face.

Something was not right, Roe thought. It had taken them much longer to reach the southern shores. While he tried to figure out where they were, Pomii ran up to him and grabbed him by his shoulders.

"Do you know what you have done?" he asked with terror in his eyes. "You have stranded us on Castle Valvatine Island, and this is the week of the full moons!"

CHAPTER 18

The orange light of a new day washed over Castle Valvatine Island as two hundred wide eyes strained through the mist for a glimpse of the shore. The mariners and the soldiers that sailed past the island did not speak a word. While the sun grew in intensity, the people aboard the ship relaxed a little and began to move about freely.

"There!" came a cry of alarm.

On the shoreline, illuminated by the rising sun, stood a black silhouette that seemed to draw all light into it. The effect on the crew was to scramble and scream wards and charms against evil spirits with a frantic straining at the oars to distance themselves from the island.

The lone Yaoite on sentry duty allowed himself a smirk as he rejoined his companions. Roe and Pomii continued to sleep while the Yaoite warriors took turns as lookouts. When the sun had turned from orange to yellow, one of the Yaoites darted off deeper into the island following a nod from the other, who remained watching the passing ship. A total of three ships had silently passed the island before the Yaoite returned from his inspection of the island; they were alone.

When the sun had reached its pinnacle, Roe began to regain consciousness. Looking down at his wound, he noticed it had closed completely and was only slightly sore. In fact, he noticed that many of the aches and pains he had gained over the years were gone. Pomii sat up and stretched in the warmth; he, too, seemed to have recovered from his injuries.

"I thought you said this place was supposed to be cursed. I haven't felt this good in years!" Roe said.

"This place operates on rules different from the rest of Nom," Pomii said as a strong wind began to whip through the forest around them. The group stared as trees were shaken and almost bent over while dust and leaves swirled toward a clear sky. While at their hiding place on the beach, not even the slightest breeze stirred the water.

A cry was heard from a small Nominious boat as the men strained against a strong current. The boat was swept to the east and around the southern tip of the island and out of sight. With a motion from Roe, one of the Yaoites sped off into the wind.

"Still think this island isn't something contrary to nature?" Pomii asked as they watched the fleeing Yaoite. While the wind whipped up around him, there was no evidence of the wind's movements in the precise area he ran in.

Dark clouds suddenly appeared over the castle, and as the party on the beach watched, they could all see a figure standing in one of the castle windows.

"I thought this place was abandoned," Roe asked the Yaoite as he watched the color drain from Pomii's face. Using hand signals, the Yaoite warrior told Roe that he had scouted the island and found no signs of inhabitance. Keeping an eye on the castle, the party began scavenging the shoreline. When the sun started to make its way toward the horizon, the Yaoite returned from watching the Nominious boat. Upon his arrival, the wind ceased, and the clouds vanished over the castle.

"He says the boat was overturned, and six soldiers managed to make their way to land," Roe told Pomii. "The boat was washed ashore farther down in a lagoon. He hid it from the soldiers and said that it looked undamaged. We should be able to use it to get off this island, but we would need to get past the soldiers, who are all armed."

As night descended and the twin moons shone in the western sky, they considered the best route to the boat. Directly to the east lay the forest thick with undergrowth and where strange sounds could be heard. It was decided that it was best to avoid the woods with the unpredictable weather. The other option was to swim out and then circle back towards the lagoon, but Pomii reminded them of the swift current that had swept the boat ashore in the first place.

The final option was to go to the castle and hope the courtyard provided a way to connect to the beach east of the soldiers' position without needing to enter the forest. With the image of the ghost in the window firmly in mind, nobody wanted to pursue that plan. As a storm began to form and cover the light of the two moons, the group decided to make for the castle anyway.

* * *

No sooner had they arrived than Pomii yanked Roe's arm as he let out a frantic, "Look!"

The two stared in horror at the shadow of a man outlined against the castle walls, where clearly no man was visible in the fading light. As Roe crept closer, he thought he heard Pomii swear something about the stupidity of Southerners. As they arrived at the wall, the shadow slowly moved off in the direction of the courtyard; they heard someone walking on sand in the same direction the shadow on the wall was going. Roe's heart thudded loudly as he watched steps materialize in the soft sand before him.

While he watched, his blood chilled as the footsteps changed from those of a man into those of a wolf. Over the rising storm behind him, he heard a faint growling from the courtyard's darkest part, directly in the direction the pawprints were heading. Roe stopped and watched the prints tread off into the darkness as he became aware of two disembodied red eyes glaring at him. As the growling became louder, he watched as those eyes emerged from the darkness.

They hovered about a foot above the ground, and with a flash of lightning, Roe momentarily made out a mutilated semi-transparent form of a man-wolf creature. As the storm increased, Roe slowly began to back away as more red glaring eyes appeared, blocking their path forward.

CHAPTER 19

The Nominious soldiers had built a massive fire on the beach, partly to shelter them from the storm and partly to ward off anything on the island. Looking down the beach to the west, they saw two men in guards' uniforms running alongside two others clothed in rags heading directly for them. The soldiers braced themselves, raising their lances and spears, but the four ran past them.

Looking in the direction they fled, the soldiers saw a dark cloud with red eyes chasing them. From the center of the cloud, angry barking and yelling were heard. Without waiting a second longer, they grabbed their gear and chased after the four. They followed them into the forest's center but lost sight of them in the darkness. Coming to a halt as the sounds disappeared, the soldiers hid in the foliage and waited.

As the cloud of men-wolves searched the beach, Roe watched the six Nominious soldiers directly in front of him. With a signal to the two Yaoites, they moved in behind the nearest soldier and subdued him. Distributing his weapons, they moved towards the next man, but when they attacked him, a bolt of lightning illuminated their struggle, and his companion sounded an alarm just before Roe ended him.

The remaining soldiers turned from watching the scene on the beach and viciously defended themselves. Moments later, they joined their companions on the ground. No sooner had they been stripped of their gear than Roe asked what had happened to the first soldiers.

With a start, Pomii pointed to the man being consumed by the forest vines. Roe signaled for the Yaoite to show them where he hid the boat as the storm raged over the island.

The group fled through the forest with a mighty effort not to fall into the choking vines. Upon reaching the lagoon, they hurriedly uncovered the boat as the sound of howling descended upon them. Roe made Pomii get into the boat as he and the Yaoites pushed it out into the choppy waves. No sooner had they all gotten aboard than the waves brought them crashing back to the beach, where the man-wolves were waiting.

The warriors swung their swords and spears with all their might to no effect as invisible jaws and claws gouged fresh wounds. Finally managing to push the boat out a second time, the group paddled to break away from land with all their strength. What seemed like hours later, they reached open waters, and instantly the night was calm. Just as they began to relax, Pomii pointed out that they were picking up speed as they remembered the strong current that ran along the south of the island.

Straining to break free, they rowed with the last of their energy as the northern shore came into sight. Hours later, the exhausted group made landfall. While they rested, they began to notice the burning of their wounds. Upon closer inspection, they discovered a green ooze forming in each wound.

Pomii directed them to find a plant with long leaves that had barbs on its edges called a Bega plant. He warned them to avoid the roots and showed them how to break open the thick leaves and extract the clear, sticky syrup. Wrapping the wounds with strips of cloth, the cooling, numbing effect was almost instantaneous.

"My friends," Roe said, addressing the Yaoites. "Report to Yao and tell him to bring as many warriors as possible. I will remain here with my brother and learn more about the Northern kingdom so we can develop the best plan of attack."

Wordlessly the Yaoites shed their Nominious armor and began the long journey towards the eastern seaboard where their boats were hidden. No sooner had they left than Roe and Pomii heard the sound of troops marching towards them from the beach. Deciding to blend in with the soldiers, the two waited until the main force had passed before following the last carts. Believing they had succeeded in their ploy, they froze with the shout—

"You, stop!" Lieutenant Voltaire commanded. "Just what do you think you are doing dressing that Zuzax native up in Nominious armor?"

CHAPTER 20

Within a palace at the center of the land overseen by house Nominious, a guard smoothed out his flawless uniform and adjusted his medals and ribbons for the third time. He waited to be admitted to the grand room where Noble Brassmas Nominious was entertaining Duke Ashwind of Dular. While there was never a good time to deliver bad news, he had drawn the short straw. With the campaign underway, Brassmas had insisted that he be informed immediately of every detail change. As midnight approached, he was finally admitted but was motioned to the side while Ashwind spoke.

"We have just heard back from the campaign, and it appears that the Northerners are more resilient than we credit them for," he said, accepting a glass of wine from Brassmas.

"How many mercenaries did you deploy?" he asked, walking over to warm himself by the fire as the storm grew in intensity outside.

"Given what we know about the state of affairs at the northern castle, I felt that four squads of eight would be sufficient to catch the palace guards unaware before they could form a significant resistance."

"But they were unsuccessful," Brassmas said, still facing the fire. "What can you tell me about the assault?"

"Well," the duke said, rising from his seat to pace the floor, "the first squad never reported back, so we assumed they were either killed or captured. The second and third squads were deployed at the same time, but one of them wandered into something described as a 'blue land' and never returned. Lieutenant Voltaire ordered everybody to stay clear of that area." Ashwind stopped pacing as he watched the lavender clouds momentarily flash to life.

"Captain Monicum reports that your mercenaries have shown themselves exemplary in every way. It's unfortunate that they haven't been more successful, but our plans will continue," Brassmas said as he turned from the fireplace and regarded the duke.

"And what is the fate of the remaining squads?"

Turning from the window as a torrent of rain pelted the hazy glass, the duke drained the last of his wine before answering.

"The remaining squads will continue to study the castle defenses, and if they find a weakness, they have orders to infiltrate and kill as many of the commanders as possible. If they don't see an opening, they must report to your Captain Monicum with detailed information on their findings."

The noble sighed as he refilled his guest's glass.

"Expanding our lands to the north was the mission of my predecessor that was denied by our king just before his untimely demise five years ago. With the Sovans out of the way, we will now be free to—"

With a sound and a nod from the duke, Brassmas finally noticed the guard.

"Yes?" he asked with a glare, taking a seat.

"Your nobleness was asked to be informed about the prisoners, sir."

"And? Well, speak up, man. What have you learned?" he asked as his foot began tapping.

"Well, the thing is, sir, they have escaped," the guard said, straightening his coat again.

"How dare you come to me and report your incompetence," Brassmas said, jumping to his feet.

"I regret to inform your nobleness, sir, but they killed the questioner in the process."

The guard braced himself as a wine glass shattered on the wall next to his head.

"Get out!" Brassmas yelled. As soon as he had left, he summoned a page.

"Have that guard flogged and hung publicly at the entrance to the dungeons."

While the page hurried off, the duke offered him another glass.

"Everybody knows that the Yaoites are solely in the service of the Sovans. It would not behoove our plans for them to come to their aid."

"What do you propose?" Brassmas asked, taking a sip of his wine while watching the duke.

"I believe I will send a battalion to Yaoite Island and eliminate their future consideration by the Sovans," the duke said as he raised his glass in a toast.

"And I believe I will tell my troops to advance on the Northern castle. With the eyes of the kingdom watching our invasion of the north and while the other houses prepare for the Contest of Kings, now is the perfect time to launch our campaign against House Kastlet."

Chapter 21

The cry came at noon, just before the farmers took their rest from the heat of the day to enjoy a light meal and a nap in the cool shade.

"FIRE!"

Regent Maxwell hurried to the area just south of the castle where they stored a good deal of their provisions. He filled and passed out water buckets for the next hour while directing his court officials to remove everything flammable from the immediate area. His black skin stood in contrast to those gathered. Those from the Forest of Thebes boasted of having the darkest complexion of anyone in Nom.

After they contained the fire, he dragged his feet towards his chambers to rid himself of his burnt clothes. Upon entering the castle, he allowed his thoughts to return to the two people absent in helping quench the fire: his younger brother Citan and his niece Lilith. Entering the throne room, he began to call for them, but a cry from the back courtyard sent him running down the northern hallway.

Princess Lilith rushed through the vestibule door that led to the throne room, then immediately slammed it shut, latching it. Breathing hard, she wiped the blood from her face onto the sleeve of her torn robe while clutching her short sword in the other.

"Lilith!" Maxwell called as he rushed over to her. As the oldest brother of Citan and Elgin, he had overseen the business affairs of the kingdom after his youngest brother's passing.

"Don't worry, Uncle Maxwell; I didn't get hurt when the other guys bled on me."

"Just what do you think you were doing fighting? That's what Citan and his men are for."

"Well, I was sitting in the garden studying works on how to be a proper lady when these two men wearing strange armor and carrying scary weapons started to climb over the wall. I just happened to have my bow with me and decided to help them down. After the first one fell in a mess, I ran over to see if I could render aid, but when I knelt to check on his wounds, I think I placed my shin on his neck, and after a gurgling sound, he quit moving."

"Lilith, you didn't!" Maxwell gasped.

"I learned a valuable lesson: never give someone aid while leaning on their windpipe; it doesn't work."

"Just what do you think your uncle Citan would say about you fighting?" Maxwell asked.

"Uncle Citan would want to know how you got your sword bloody," Citan said, walking into the vestibule from the throne room. Fresh wounds were seen through his torn garments.

"When I turned to offer my royal aid to the second scary man, he tried to swipe at me with his sword. I don't think guys with twelve arrows in them should try to fight sword maidens; it just gets messy," Lilith said.

While Citan looked with pride at his niece, Maxwell walked away in a huff.

"This is just the first wave," Citan called after his brother. "They tried to surprise us with a mercenary attack; then, a full-scale siege will commence in the next couple of days."

"Our guards cannot hold off a siege. I suggest we relocate to our pavilion in Celestias so we can use our ships if we need to," Maxwell said as he collected several of his parchments from the large table in the back of the throne room.

Ignoring his brother, Citan studied the model of their castle that he and Lilith had built to scale on the table. Underneath the castle was a topographical map of the Northern kingdom that identified the settlements of the Zuzax people and the royal harbor to the north that still held a very strong criminal presence.

"Do we know who these invaders are?" Maxwell asked.

"They are from House Dular," Lilith said with a smile. At seventeen years of age, there were few times that she knew something that her uncles didn't.

"That's right," Citan said. "They had markings on their body indicating they belonged to a Dular mercenary unit."

"And I think this settles the question of who the better warrior is," Lilith said, examining one of Citan's wounds. "I was able to defend our domain without getting a boo-boo."

"And while you dispatched your two, something I am very proud of you for, by the way, I dealt with six others," Citan said as he pushed some of Maxwell's parchments aside and placed a red block on the map just to the south of the castle before a mountain pass.

"Our scouts report a troop of Nominious soldiers about a day's ride from here."

"Nominious? Not Belthane? Why are the Dular and Nominious forces attacking us?" Maxwell asked.

"That I cannot answer, but we should stay and defend what is ours. This castle can survive under siege for three full months, four if we ration our provisions, and that would be the practical approach," Citan said.

"The practical approach would be to gather as much of our provisions as possible and make our way to the port of Celestias. That fire destroyed about a month's worth of provisions."

"A month?" Citian asked. "Supposing we were to go north, we would need at least a week to do that. Sure, we could get ourselves and some of our people out today, but most of them would be left behind, and that's something neither of us is willing to do."

"We could send to Celestias for help. Because who wouldn't want to help the royal family in their hour of need?" Lilith asked. "I'll bet that if you asked, that entire town would be tripping over each other for the opportunity to come to our aid. What better way to ingratiate yourself to the royal family than by pulling their fat out of the fire?"

"Well," Maxwell said, moving towards his favorite chair but pausing as he looked at his filthy clothes. "We are going to need all of the help we can get. While I go change, would you like to select a messenger?" he asked Citan.

Moments later, Lilith and Citan watched as their messenger rode out of the city gates. Suddenly, three arrows assaulted him from alongside the road, and he fell from his runner beast.

"Guards!" Citan yelled. "It appears that there are still some mercenaries to contend with."

Chapter 22

Roe made his way over to Lieutenant Voltaire while indicating Pomii.

"I caught this Zuzax scout last night impersonating our troops, and I am taking him to Captain Monicum."

"Then why isn't he tied up?" the lieutenant asked.

"I knew I forgot something," Roe said, swinging with all his might for Voltaire's jaw. As his head snapped back, the two watched his eyes roll back in his head as he fell to the ground. Without waiting for further discovery, Pomii wrapped a cloth around his face before donning a helmet.

As the battalion made its way north, nobody further challenged them. After a day of walking, a horrible stench of death and decay arose as they approached the blue land. Climbing the ridge that skirted the area, Pomii wept as he saw the remains of the six-legged creature the soldiers had slain.

"No doubt one of them took its head for a trophy," Roe said.

That night, as the Nominious army set up camp preparing for the morning's raid on the castle, Roe and Pomii inched their way closer to the commander's tent.

"What are we doing here?" Pomii asked. "I don't like pretending I am a Southern soldier, and while I love Grammy, I think she made a terrible call to keep our people away from the castle. Emperor Elgin has been nothing but kind to our people, and he has given us more protection from Southerners than anybody. I think that if Grammy had just thought about it for a moment after Aunt Cleo's death, she wouldn't have made that decision."

"My family is no friend of House Nominious, that's for sure. I want to get a good idea of how things are going so I can report to Yao when he comes. Hiding here just might be the best way to do that," said Roe.

"You didn't know this, but I am an earth talker. I can communicate to my people through the earth as long as someone is out there listening," Pomii said.

"I have never heard of such a thing. Can you talk to Yaoite Island? Maybe I can get a message out that way."

"No, the water would stop it. Grammy is the only one who can communicate across the sea."

"That was spectacular!" Roe said. "Do you think you could teach me to be an earth talker?"

"I don't know; we started learning to listen to the earth before we could walk."

A commotion from the north end of the camp raised spears and unsheathed swords. Moments later, four bruised and battered Dular mercenaries stumbled into camp. After food and water had been brought, and their wounds tended to by the medics, they told of their attempted raid.

"Our squad was selected to create a distraction while the others snuck into the castle. We went to their food supply warehouse around noon and waited until it was mostly empty—"

"Why didn't you wait for nightfall?" asked Captain Monicum.

"If they waited until nightfall, they couldn't strike all of their military leaders at once," Lieutenant Voltaire replied.

"Our plan was for our squad to start a big enough fire that it would require everybody to put it out. While that was happening, the other squad would sneak into their base and ambush them in return. When they did get back, they would be tired from the fire, and we would have both the element of surprise and vitality on our side.

"We went to the warehouse exactly as planned and split up into two teams: one fire starter and one lookout. We had a blaze going in five buildings by the time they responded. It took them the rest of the afternoon to contain the blaze, but our other squad never rejoined us that night. As we waited, we saw a messenger sent from the castle, and we intervened," he said, holding up a parchment. "The message was to their forces in the northern port of Celestia asking to come to support them. Not long after we intercepted the messenger, we saw a strike party coming our way from the castle, so we set an ambush. As it turned out, though, we were meant to see them. No sooner had we gathered on both sides of the road than we were attacked from behind. What you see here is all that is left of us."

While the surviving mercenaries were talking, Roe and Pomii concealed themselves near the commander's tent and listened. After they had given their account, the captain and lieutenant conferred inside.

"This battle may not end as soon as we would like it to," Captain Monicum began. "This is supposed to be a simple slaughter with nothing opposing us other than the personal guards of some merchants. How were they tough enough to kill twenty-eight of your mercenaries?"

"I would give you answers if I had them," Lieutenant Voltaire began, "and as I have made known to you, I discovered two spies within our ranks earlier."

"Spies that it would have been nice to interrogate had you captured them."

"There were complications. Still, there was something familiar about them . . ." said Voltaire.

"Regardless, with the second battalion making landfall even as we speak, we need a swift and decisive victory here. Our forces back home are counting on us."

"I don't see Kastlet being that much of a concern. Our troops should have things sufficiently wrapped up without too much trouble. After all, how much opposition can a few fishermen present?" asked Voltaire.

"How much opposition can a few merchants' guards present?"

There was silence as the two sat contemplating the upcoming battle.

"You know," Monicum began, "we have a resource at our disposal who is quite familiar with this castle. I think I will message the homeland and ask for King Slayer. You may know him as Lefterry."

Chapter 23

An hour past midnight, the lights in the commander's tent winked out. Tonight, there had been no island song to quell the savage lands. As an uneasy stillness settled on the invading camp, two shadows crept into the commander's tent and over to the sleeping captain. Withdrawing a rag covered in the pain-numbing Bega root salve, the first shadow covered the captain's nose and mouth. After a brief struggle, they muzzled and rolled him up in a blanket before tying ropes around it.

Wordlessly, they loaded the captain onto the back of one of the three runner beasts before leading them through the high grass surrounding the camp. Once they had gained sufficient distance, the two shadows mounted their beasts and followed a ravine toward the castle. They had barely covered thirty paces before encountering a thin rope across their paths that knocked them off of their mounts.

"Well, what do we have here?" Lieutenant Voltaire said to the two marauders accompanying him. "I knew you spies would try to report back to your commander, so I set several traps on either side of the road."

Pomii grabbed a handful of stones and flung them toward the runner beasts, startling them. Leaping on the back of the nearest one, he turned the battle-trained beast upon the nearest marauder. As the dust flew into the air, Roe attacked the man closest to him with all the skill and savagery he could summon. Lieutenant Voltaire grabbed Roe's runner beast and fled from the fight.

"He will bring more soldiers," Pomii said, looking down at the mangled marauder. "And we cannot outrun them if one of us is walking."

Roe listened for a minute before signaling for his brother to wait for him. Hurrying off into the darkness, he soon returned with his runner beast.

"Lieutenant Voltaire really was good at making traps. He won't be bothering us anymore, though."

Making haste with their precious cargo, they journeyed uninterrupted through the remainder of the night until the sun began to break upon the Northern kingdom. Leaving the tall grass, they continued their journey toward the castle on the main road. As the castle came into sight, they slowed their pace and began to relax.

Roe barely managed to dodge a spear hurled from the bushes. Instantly drawing his sword as his attacker knocked him from his mount, he leaped to his feet and met a dark-skinned man dressed in purple and black merchant's clothes. The man displayed a row of perfectly white teeth as he swatted Roe's attack away with ease and countered with an attack of his own. Roe deflected, then parried, but the merchant grabbed his wrist and knocked his sword out of his hand. Roe grabbed the front of the man's clothes, flipped him in the air, slammed him to the ground, and placed his knife at his throat.

"Surrender, or your friend dies," the man said with a smile never leaving his face.

Roe glanced to where the other merchants had surrounded Pomii, and as he did, the man smashed a rock into the side of his head, causing him to crumple to the ground.

* * *

Roe woke to find the same face before him with the same irritating smile. Attempting to stand, he discovered that his arms and legs were shackled.

"You are the most curious prisoner this dungeon has ever seen, but we have rules about what to do with deserters."

"We aren't deserters," Roe said, squeezing his eyes closed.

"You are a Southerner wearing Nominious armor, ride their mounts, and accompany their captain. But where are my manners? My name is Citan."

"I am Roe of the Yaoites."

"A Yaoite? That explains your fighting style. The last person to hold a blade to my throat was a pirate with a decade of battles behind him. It was the last thing he ever did. So, tell me, Roe of the Yaoites, what is a sword for hire doing in my brother's kingdom?"

"The Zuzax magistrate asked for our help against the marauders."

"Hmm," Citan said, studying Roe for a moment. "I find your story incredible. It is common knowledge that the Yaoites work exclusively for one of the houses of the Southern kingdoms. Would you have me believe that you are going against the other houses and defending the Zuzax tribe, who want nothing to do with my kingdom by bringing me the captain of the Nominious army?" Citan threw back his head and had a good belly laugh.

"It's true. We thought you would appreciate having your enemy in your possession."

"Oh, I do; believe me, I do. But I still think you are deserters. You are a Southerner, and I have never met a Yaoite who was a Southerner. I think you tire of the army life, and after hearing stories of the north from a Zuzax slave, you freed him and made your way to us. You probably were the personal guard to the captain here; that's why you could have captured him alive and why you have some skill in fighting."

"That's a lie, but even if it was true, why are we in chains?" Roe asked.

"As I said, we have laws about deserters. Once a person has betrayed his country and house, how can we ever trust the outsider? If he has turned his back on his people, what fealty can we expect from a person like that?"

"I request to speak to your emperor."

"I see. You find it improbable that a person such as I can be a person of influence?" Citan asked.

"The only person I have ever heard of who left the merchants guild and became a ruler is Emperor Elgin. Do you want me to believe that you have done this, even though you wear merchant's clothing?"

Citan gave another belly laugh as he stood.

"Very well, I will see if our *empress* has time for you. We are planning for a siege, as you know."

Looking around the dungeon, Roe spotted the unconscious body of his brother. After several calls, Pomii slowly regained consciousness. Looking around the cell, he tried the limits of his chains.

"Brother, this is becoming a habit," he said.

Roe filled him in on his conversation with Citan as they waited.

"Are you going to do that twist chain thing?"

"No, I want to see if we can make an ally of these people," Roe said.

A few moments later, they heard the key in their door as Citan returned.

"As I suspected, the empress is not willing to review your case and challenge the law of the land with the siege underway and all."

"What will happen to us then?" Pomii asked.

"In accordance with our laws, all traitors are to be executed."

CHAPTER 24

Ivan Sovan ignored his breakfast as he met with the elders and directed the clerks in preparation for the Contest of Kings. Since Leotan's murder, he had assumed control of the kingdom as a regent. He had spent every waking moment following through on the affairs of state while overseeing preparations for the contest. He had spent days with the scribes, combing through the laws in search of the proper procedure for a murdered sovereign. Was the regent to become the next sovereign, as in the case of the reigning sovereign dying on the field of battle?

House Nominious and Dular fiercely opposed that understanding. Since there was nothing in the laws stating that he automatically ascended the throne, it was determined that another Contest of Kings be held.

Under normal circumstances, the contest was to occur every five years, and each of the five houses would present its best candidate for a sovereign. A series of contests were held to determine their candidate's adequacy. The contests lasted five days, and on the sixth day, the council of elders met behind closed doors to determine the next sovereign. They met to confer what the next age would require of them, given the next sovereign's strengths and weaknesses.

The elders had served the royal courts in various capacities, anywhere from clerks or scribes to former sovereigns, before being allowed to become an elder. The only requirements were that they renounce any ties to their family house and that they exceeded the age of sixty-five.

With all of the preparations that had demands on his time, the heaviest burden he carried was his absence from his own brother's funeral and his unresolved death.

"No, no, no. Kastlet cannot follow Belthane in the test of wisdom literature. They would be very insulted at the prospect, and things are tense enough as it is," Elder Mattias said. "You must consider the size of each house in that test."

"Size doesn't seem a very good indicator of wisdom, Elder."

"I am here to help you, Regent Ivan; I don't have time to argue with you about custom," Mattias replied.

A sharp rap on the chamber doors before a clerk entered and hurried over to Ivan. After he whispered a message, Ivan excused himself, ignoring the elders' complaints.

Exiting the chamber, he found his sister-in-law, Lady Lynn, waiting for him.

"I am sorry to pull you away from state affairs, but I just learned that Yaoite Island has been destroyed."

"*What*!? How did that happen? Who is responsible for this?" Ivan asked.

"We received a report that warships began firing on the island yesterday morning."

"Why are you waiting till now to tell me?"

"I tried to send word as soon as I learned of the attack, but the messenger never got through to you. That's why I have come myself," Lynn said.

"Do we know who is responsible? Are there any survivors? How did you hear about this?"

"I sent another messenger to Yao, asking him to avenge my husband's death. When the messenger returned, he said that the ships he saw belonged to House Kastlet, but when he reached the island, Dular soldiers were everywhere. What does all this mean?" Lynn asked.

"It may mean that the houses are conspiring against us. If what we suspect is true and Lefterry did murder Leotan, well, it's no secret that House Nominious employed the assassin. The investigation into Leotan's death is just one more matter I need to clear before the next sovereign is determined. If the next sovereign is from House Nominious, we may never get answers," Ivan said.

"Regent!" a messenger called as he hurried over. "House Kastlet requests that you visit their lands immediately."

"They do, do they? You may inform Christoff that even though I am only a regent, I am serving as the sovereign, and if there is a message he has for me, he can come here to deliver it," Ivan said before the messenger hurried off.

"Regent Ivan, Elder Mattias is insisting you return to chambers," a clerk informed him.

"It never stops," Ivan said, turning from Lady Lynn.

"Make sure to get some rest when you can, Ivan. You look like you haven't slept in a year."

* * *

The next day as he continued with the preparations, Ivan received an official summons from the Count of Kastlet, who had just arrived at the capitol.

What's this guy's problem? I have matters of the kingdom to attend to, Ivan thought as he made his way toward the palace owned by the Kastlets.

"Regent Ivan here to see Count Christoff," the herald announced as Ivan pushed his way into the meeting room.

"Count Christoff, how may I be of service to you?"

"I am told you received my message yesterday," Christoff said with a glare.

"Yes, I did but due to—"

"Maybe you thought that you had something more important going on than to answer an official request."

"Apologies, my count, there was—"

"Do you realize the inconvenience you have caused a reigning member of one of the five houses—"

"Count Christoff, you will be silent while I am speaking. Is that understood?" Ivan shouted. "I am not your subordinate, and I don't answer to your whims. I am the regent sovereign of the Island of the Mighty, something you would do well to remember unless you would like me to hold you in contempt and ensure that your house receives the least consideration in the upcoming Contest of Kings. Are we clear?"

Count Christoff glared at Ivan as the royal guards prepared to intervene. Finally, Christoff sat back in his chair, defeated.

"If it pleases the court," Christoff continued in a much quieter voice, "I would request the presence of the regent to ascertain the growing threat I am facing on my borders."

"What news is this?" Ivan asked, taking a seat. "I have heard of no invasion upon this land."

"The invasion doesn't come from without but from within."

"Please be careful, Count Christoff. It sounds like you are accusing the other houses of treason."

"That is precisely what I am saying. The armies of House Nominious are gathered on my northern border while the armies of House Dular are gathered to the east."

"This will have to be verified by a court official, of course," Ivan said. "On the other hand, I have verified knowledge that the armies of the two aforementioned houses are engaged in campaigns in the Northern kingdom. It seems improbable that they would be fighting on two fronts while committing an act of treason."

"I realize that a claim of this magnitude needs to be verified by a court official, hence my request to you yesterday," the count said.

"Christoff, I don't doubt your integrity, but I must complete a month's worth of preparations before the week's end. I am shackled to my responsibilities as a regent preparing for the Contest of Kings. I am truly sorry."

"Not as sorry as I am," Christoff said as he left the room.

CHAPTER 25

The door swung open as four guards entered the cell. Wordlessly, they unfastened Pomii's chains and escorted him out. Upon reaching the throne room, Lilith handed him a massive fruit and told him to stand still. Walking across the room, she picked up her bow and notched three arrows.

"Ah, Princess, hold on. I just wanted—"

"*Princess?* I think you mean *Empress.* It comes with having your dad, the emperor, die in celebration of the anniversary of your fiancé's death. Now hold still; this is my first time shooting three arrows at once."

Pomii closed his eyes as all the color drained out of his face. Seconds later, he was covered in stickiness as the fruit exploded. Dropping the remains and checking himself for wounds, he listened to Lilith's laugh.

"Silly boy, there were no tips on those arrows. Why would I want to harm my newfound podium?"

"You're crazy," he stammered.

"I know, isn't it grand? But now that you have helped me with my shooting, what can I do for you, Zuzax-person-turned-soldier-turned-trader?"

"There has been a misunderstanding," Pomii began as he explained his entire encounter with Roe. He ended by showing her his star scar.

"That's fascinating. You know, what's also fascinating is the amount of time it takes for the Nominious troops to lay siege to this castle. Come with me," Lilith said, walking out across the balcony.

The two stood there watching as the invading army constructed ramps.

"Our chemnotist was able to find the right amount of chemicals and mesmerizers to affect the captain. We have learned that this is just the first wave sent to establish a base camp. Right now, there are about two hundred soldiers outside this castle. The rest of the battalion is still in the mountain pass and should be here tomorrow, but we are already prepared for them. Now come with me."

Taking him to the model of the castle, she indicated the area to the east of the castle.

"There is a second battalion heading around the mountain range to the east, directly towards Zuzax nation. Now, should your guys get back to Yaoite Island and should they send help before the Nominious forces arrive, and should they beat them, well, that would be an interesting battle."

"I need to get back to my people," Pomii said.

Ignoring him, Lilith continued. "My sources tell me that there are over one thousand soldiers in each battalion. Do you know how many merchant guards I have with me? Slightly over two hundred. I know this castle; we can hold out for a while. But what happens when that 'for a while' runs out? Have you thought about this? No, of course not. Why would you? You are just a tribesperson trying to get back to his people, the same people who have rejected my family and me in case you had forgotten," Lilith said, fixing Pomii with a cold stare.

"If all you are doing is preparing for the worst, what good does it do you to keep my brother here and me? Hasn't the information you learned from the captain been enough to let us go?" Pomii asked.

"And where would you go if I released you?"

"We would return to the Zuzax and help them prepare for the Nominious army."

"Oh, I see," Lilith said. "All this time, I have been explaining my situation to you, and all you can think of is going back to Grammy, who still hates us, and you would just leave us to burn?"

"Princess—"

"*Empress!*"

"I apologize, empress. I know you would never abandon your lands, especially if they were about to be invaded—"

"Let me just stop you right there before you compare my decisions to yours. You have never had the weight of an entire realm on your shoulders before."

Pomii held her gaze for as long as he could before hanging his head, knowing there was an imminent threat to his people while being helpless to warn them or stand by them. What did Lilith expect from him?

"When will your Northern forces arrive from Celestia?" Pomii finally asked. "What if Roe and I stay to help you fight the invasion until they arrive? Could we go help our people then?"

"They aren't even aware of the situation."

"Well, couldn't you just send a messenger to ask them to come?" Pomii asked.

"What a brilliant idea; why didn't I think of that?"

"I mean, it would about double the number of guards you have here, but at the same time, it would leave the town defenseless against all of the criminals in the Southern kingdom, so I could see why you wouldn't want to do that," Pomii said.

"Brilliant! If we had but sent a messenger to the north when we were first invaded, our guards should have been able to arrive back just in time. What a remarkable grasp of the obvious you have there, Pomii! Simply wonderful. Somebody free this man from his chains."

"You have already sent the messenger, haven't you?" Pomii asked.

"And we watched all of them fall right before our eyes."

Taking a step closer to the empress, he brought himself up as straight as possible.

"We'll go but on the condition that the Northern troops aid the Zuzax people. You said it yourself; the second battalion is headed straight for my tribe. Wouldn't it be of greater benefit to the Northern kingdom and the Zuzax tribe to stop them before they get here?"

Lilith weighed the argument for a full minute.

"I am not interested in watching another messenger die," she concluded. "Even if it is a traitor."

"That won't be us. We have broken out of the Nominious dungeon, escaped Valvatine Island, captured a captain, and we will succeed in getting to Celestias."

"Oh really? And just how do you plan on doing that?"

"From what you indicated, your messengers took the eastern route to the north. We will take the western route," Pomii said.

"You know the blue land extends west of this castle, right?"

"I am Zuzax; I know the paths through the blue lands that outsiders don't."

The briefest of smiles appeared on Lilith's lips for a fraction of a second. "I will allow you to make the journey, but you alone. It's not like you would need an *outsider's* help through the blue lands and in preparation for the impending battle. As for Roe, I have plans for him. I need to get into the practice of slaying Southerners."

Chapter 26

The generals stood smiling as black smoke rolled past them from the castle below. It had been a short campaign, and victory was almost a guarantee. Fighting had been minimal, but the inhabitants were more seafarers and not battle-hardened soldiers. They watched as a small stream of non-combatants fled for their lives along the route that would eventually lead them to their ships. There was still a slight concern, though—the ruler of this land was unaccounted for; it was possible that he lay among the fallen. Regardless, between the two armies that would split his land, one thing was sure: he would never reign again.

* * *

"Count Christoff to see Regent Ivan," the court herald announced.

"Tell him I am busy," Ivan replied before the herald started off. "No, wait. Ask him to join me for dinner and impress upon him that is my soonest availability."

Ivan had slept maybe four hours since their last meeting, and the contest was less than twenty-four hours away.

"Regent Ivan, how many times do I have to tell you that the proper order of procession is first, the Monarch's Statement, *then* the playing of our national anthem, and then, *lastly*, the procession. The Monarch's Statement is given *in advance* of the anthem because that is what draws everyone together so we can show proper respect *for* the anthem," said Elder Johannes.

"You're right; my apologies. Once the procession is completed, all the houses will be officially gathered, and then I will address them with the Monarch's Statement once I have finished writing it."

"No, you weren't listening!" Elder Lucas said. "And why haven't you finished the speech yet? You have had ten days to work on a five-minute speech. One would think the honor of commanding the attention of all five families at once would be a greater concern for you."

As four elders hurried around the table to finish the arrangements, Ivan fell into his overstuffed chair as he fought to keep his eyes open.

"Regent Ivan, I demand an audience, and I will not tolerate further delay," Count Christoff yelled as he entered the room, accompanied by his guards, all of whom had their swords drawn, the smell of smoke thick on their clothes.

"What is this?" Elder Mattias asked. "To barge into the throne room with weapons drawn is an act of treason against the crown!"

Undaunted, Christoff shoved the elder to the floor and drew his sword, pointing it at Ivan's throat.

"I tried to warn you, but you were too busy, and now my land lies in ruins thanks to your negligence."

"Christoff, I am truly sorry—"

"No, it's too late for that. It's too late for anything," Christoff said, tossing his sword on the table. Pulling out a chair, he tossed the parchments it contained to the floor as the elders gasped. Only then could Ivan see the tear-stained streaks through the soot on his face.

Rising, he signaled the palace guards to leave as he turned to address the elders.

"Elders and learned men of the high court, today one of our five houses has fallen, and I am to blame. Count Christoff has come seeking aid while I personally have been unable to verify the acts Houses Nominious and Dular have committed against House Kastlet.

"As of this moment," Ivan continued, "by the powers vested in me as regent of the Island of the Mighty, I am suspending the Contest of Kings until this matter is satisfactorily resolved and justice has been restored to House Kastlet."

"You can't just dismiss all the timing and preparations that have gone into this event," Elder Lucas began as all the other elders voiced their concerns at once.

"SILENCE. My decision is firm. Send a message to the standing army; we march for Kastlet tonight."

* * *

Ivan woke to the gentle nudging of General Amis.

"All is ready, my lord, but I must advise you to reconsider going. The facts have already been established; there's no need for the regent to abandon his position at the capitol."

Pushing his general aside, he fumbled to fasten his sword belt. After several moments, he thrust it to the chair from where he had just risen.

"It is the job of the regent to lead the standing army into battle," Ivan began.

"Respectfully, sir, that's what your generals are for."

"This is what I want you to do," Ivan said, picking up his sword belt and trying to fasten it again.

"I will send Christoff with the Royal Navy to the Nominious shores. Meanwhile, I want you to withdraw the Sovan soldiers from the standing army, combine them with our palace soldiers back on our lands, and attack House Dular from the west. While stationed on Kastlet lands, I will send the royal army south to engage both houses at the Kastlet palace. Without any way to retreat to their lands, the Dulars will be forced to flee to the Nominious lands. We will trap them both there with our royal army and the navy," Ivan said as he finally managed to fasten his sword belt.

"Regent Ivan, I implore you to take a moment to reconsider. If you send away the Sovan soldiers, there will be no one here to protect you, and we still haven't learned exactly how Sovereign Leotan was murdered," General Amis said.

"Leading the standing army without the support of the soldiers from your own house would put you in a dangerous position. Do you think the Dulars or the Nominious soldiers will attack their fellow citizens? Their house leaders have already committed treason; why would their soldiers remain loyal to the royal army?"

"I see your point," Ivan replied, leaning heavily on the back of his chair.

"This may be out of character for a fighting man to say, but maybe this time, the best approach to matters is a diplomatic one," Amis said as Ivan removed his sword belt.

* * *

The next day around noon, Ivan finally rose to address the courts.

"A regrettable evil has occurred in our lands. For the first time in our history, brother has betrayed brother. I have realized that a regent is not fit to resolve this matter. Therefore, we will table any further action on behalf of House Kastlet until we can crown a proper sovereign."

"You are going to regret this, Ivan!" Count Christoff yelled. "The blood of my people and family is on your negligent head. Before all the houses gathered here, I swear that your blood will stain my sword."

Chapter 27

"Let's go," Citan said, entering the dungeon. Accompanied by four guards, his customary smile was nowhere to be seen today.

As Roe was dragged through the halls towards the courtyard, he kept an eye out for Pomii. Maybe his brother had been able to secure his release at the last minute. Perhaps the warriors had returned with Yao. But upon seeing the execution block, his dwindling hope vanished.

Standing beside the block was a young woman covered in a veil, and next to her was an older version of Citan. Roe was fastened to the anchoring loop while his crime of betrayal and the law that it violated were read. It occurred to him that the very thing that had separated him from his family was the death of a Nominious noble, and now he was going to be killed for betraying that house.

"Wait," Roe said as a man with a huge axe came forth. "Will you allow the prisoner to make a final statement?"

At a nod from the veiled woman, the executioner stayed his axe.

Standing as tall as his restraints would allow, Roe stared at the two merchants.

"My name is Royce Sovan, and I am the son of the late sovereign, Leotan Sovan."

The veiled woman gasped, and, within five steps, she stood in front of him. Removing her veil, Roe looked into a familiar face from his childhood. Her skin was darker, her body thin but toned, and her eyes still were bluer than the sky. He allowed himself a smile which quickly disappeared in a slap.

"I remember you, Royce. Or is it now Roe? I remember a snot-nosed little boy who, upon learning that I was half Zuzax, asked me which half. I remember sitting in front of that same boy at one of the boring ceremonies we were required to suffer through, and once we were allowed to leave, I found out that somebody had tied my long hair in knots with the hair of the girl next to me."

Roe tried as hard as he could not to smile but failed. The fire in Lilith's eyes was unmistakable.

"I don't care who you are; we proceed as planned," Lilith said to the protests of her uncles.

"Hold him down," she instructed the executioner. "That's an order."

As Roe was pinned to the execution block, he turned and watched as Lilith herself struggled to pick up the executioner's axe. Raising it above her head, she tottered for a moment, giving a slight yelp before crashing backward. She lay there blinking for a minute; her arms fully extended above her head, still clutching the axe. Laughing as Citan helped her to her feet, she explained that she just wanted to see if she could wield that enormous axe. Seconds later, Roe was freed from his bonds.

* * *

Hours later, Roe and Pomii crept through the blue fog as they made their way north. The fog constantly changed from light to dark blue in the sunlight.

"Have you gone this way before?" Roe asked.

"You must keep your voice down; you don't want to attract any creatures," Pomii said. "The Zuzax learned long ago which shades of blue are dangerous and which are safe to travel through." He became excited upon seeing a white tree that appeared as if its bark was dripping off it. Roe noted that the blue air seemed afraid of it. Unsheathing his sword, Pomii hacked off a branch and whittled it into a straight stick. Then taking a small knife from his belt, he began to carve.

"Focus on where you want to go, not on the blue," he said, tossing a compass to Roe. "We know the direction we seek, and if a way is visible through the light blue, we proceed. If a way is clear, then it becomes obscured by the thicker blue, we change directions, but we must always keep moving. If we stop, we risk the blue becoming thicker around us, and that is when we are in danger of being pulled into the land of ever-night. Whatever else happens, our lives depend on us being out of the blue when night comes," Pomii said as he continued to carve.

Even though they continued without stopping, the sun began to set, and it became harder and harder to make out the lighter areas of blue. Pomii quickened his pace, and once, Roe completely lost all sight of him. Just as he was about to risk calling him, he suddenly appeared in front of him, urging him to make haste. The dark blue soon turned black while the sounds of animals Roe had never heard before grew closer. They stumbled through the darkness for a bit longer until a starry night sky broke overhead.

Relieved, the two sat on the ground, panting as they looked across at the twinkling lights of Celestia.

"Now that we can stop, there is something I must do."

Roe watched as Pomii dug a shallow hole in the ground and inserted one end of his stick beside the hole. Kneeling over the hole, he spoke in a language Roe didn't recognize. As he did so, Roe realized that the carvings were runes as some began to glow green while others shone red and blue.

Seconds later, he heard a voice answering Pomii from the hole. The two conversed for a minute before Pomii withdrew the stick, and the runes went dark.

"I told our people we are bringing help and not to lose heart."

"With the siege to begin at first light, we don't have a moment to lose," Roe said as he began running towards the town.

* * *

Captain Rosi, Commander of the Merchants Guard was upset at the empress's summons, especially about the part of aiding the Zuzax people instead of going to the castle. He was even more irritated about leaving the town unguarded and argued with Roe that there were still dangerous criminals that would take advantage of their absence.

It was only after Pomii had promised him the help of the Zuzax people, should any uprising occur while they were gone, that Rosi relented. As the guards lived, ready to be called into action at a moment's notice to confront an uprising, it took little time for them to mount up and ride out into the night.

The guards reached the Zuzax tribe as the sun peeked across the land, just in time to meet the oncoming Nominious soldiers. No sooner had the sun risen than the earth began to shake, and a large plume of dust was seen rising in the west toward the Northern kingdom's castle.

CHAPTER 28

"Lynn, you can't tell me you have never even considered Ivan. He certainly does know how to command a room when he enters. It's probably because he is head and shoulders taller than everyone else, but that deep voice of his, what a lady wouldn't do . . ."

Lady Lynn sat in the uppermost room of her palatial estate, entertaining her sister Ellen of House Belthane.

"Lady Ellen, the way you talk about him, someone might assume you are looking for your third husband!"

"Well, the other two were less than what a lady of my position would find desirable."

"Then why did you marry them?" Lynn asked.

"There are reasons to marry somebody other than for love, my dear Lynn. Besides, don't you find the adage 'we were in love a bit cliché? What happens when two people fall out of love? What happens when the spark has died, and reality has set in, or in some cases, a woman doesn't hold her man's attention like she used to?" Ellen asked.

"You forget, my dear sister, the one lesson you simply refuse to learn: Love is a choice. A choice that requires sacrifice, a choice that requires you to put someone else's needs and wants ahead of your own, a choice that, if made, will make all the difference in the world between two people."

"Oh Lynn, there you go getting preachy again. It would mean so much more coming from you if—"

At that moment, an alarm sounded, indicating an imminent threat. Guards rushed into the room and ushered the two ladies to the most secure room in the entire palace. Once they sealed the door, candles were lit, and things became uncomfortably silent.

"What's going on?" Ellen demanded of a young lieutenant.

"I am not sure, my lady. Upon hearing the alarm, I have standing orders to take the royalty to safety."

"So you have no idea why you grabbed us and forced us into this musky room?" Ellen demanded.

"Ellen, stop it," Lynn chided. "He is doing what he was trained to do, and you should thank him for doing his job and keeping us safe."

Turning to the young man, she asked for his name.

"My name is Julian, ma'am."

"So, tell me, Julian, do you have a way of finding out why the alarm was sounded?"

"No, ma'am, but with your permission, I can open this door and see if I can find out."

"I didn't think that was allowed," Lynn said.

"Hush, Lynn," Ellen said. "Of course, we want you to find out why we are here and get back to us as quickly as possible."

The lieutenant hurried away as silence once again settled on the bunker.

"I can't take this," Ellen said. "This quiet is killing me."

Several minutes later, another lieutenant arrived and pulled the door securely behind him.

"What happened to the other guy?" Ellen asked.

"He was relieved of his commission for abandoning his post," was the reply.

"How can that be? We told him to find out what was going on."

"Understand, ma'am, that once a soldier is committed to this bunker, nothing but an order from an executive can cause him to open that door."

"What is your name, lieutenant?" Lynn asked.

"Boltar, ma'am."

"Can you tell me, Lieutenant Boltar, why the alarm was sounded?" asked Lynn.

"All I know is that twenty raiding ships are sitting in our harbor."

"Tell me about these ships. Do they fly any colors, and if so, what kind?"

"They have black sails with red crosses on them. Our records show that that emblem has been seen leaving the location of several known slaughters," the lieutenant said.

"Lieutenant Boltar, I am ordering you, as lady of the house, to open that door and release us."

* * *

Half an hour later, Lady Lynn stood alone on the docks as one of the ships pulled up. After they had secured the moorings and extended the plank, Yao stepped forth. Lynn stooped in courtesy as Yao bowed.

"We have heard of your travesty, Master Yao, and you are most welcome in these lands. House Sovan stands ready to meet whatever needs you may have."

"You have my gratitude, Lady Lynn, but there are matters that I must attend to in the Northern kingdom. With your permission, I would like to leave some of our young and our women in your care. If that is acceptable to you, my wife Cinthia will speak on behalf of our people."

While they made arrangements, Yao gathered a select few of his finest warriors to make the journey north. As the sun began to set, the party set out, mounted on the finest runner beasts the Sovans had to offer towards the Belthane border. After a day's journey across the most fertile lands of the kingdom, their journey ended in a confrontation with the Belthane guard.

"Yao of the Yaoites, I must apologize, but I cannot allow you to proceed any further across our lands," their commander said.

Yao strode forth until his nose all but touched the commanders.

"I am under orders from Lady Lynn of House Sovan to proceed across these lands. Here is a letter with the official seal on it."

Taking several steps back, the commander cleared his throat several times before answering.

"I understand that, but we have heard from Lady Ellen, er, from an official that you are headed for the Northern kingdom, and I'm afraid that I must insist that you return by the route you came."

Yao stood staring at the commander with the note in his hand as weariness and anger competed for dominance.

"Mark my words well, Commander of the Belthanes; if you continue on this path, you will make yourself my enemy. Choose your next words wisely," Yao said.

CHAPTER 29

"I need every able body to mount up," Citan said as he knocked the dust from his clothes.

"At least give us a chance to clean up first," Lilith said as she splashed water on her face.

As soon as the entire Nominious army had entered the valley leading to the castle, Citan released the two creatures he had captured in the blue lands. He affectionately called these enormous burrowers thunder worms. They were delighted with the island's rocks and showed their gratitude by thundering. No sooner had the avalanches started than the merchant guards destroyed the advance party outside their castle.

"We need to go to the aid of the Zuzax people as soon as we can, but if you want to wash the mud from between your toes and get a pedicure, then I will bow to your judgment."

"Uncle Citan, I like it better when I am sarcastic with you and not the other way around. I can't wait to meet with Grammy and point out that the person who just saved her life is still owed sixteen birthday gifts. Can you imagine what a lady in my position could do with the secret arts of the Zuzax people? I bet she has found a way never to get tired or need sleep. She is probably only forty years old, but there were side effects, which is why she looks like she is about nine hundred.

"As my first act of empress of the Zuzax nation, I will decree that they must eliminate all side effects of their secret arts," Lilith said.

"On second thought," Citan said, "maybe you should stay back and freshen up before this long overdue reunion. After all, it wouldn't do for the empress of the Northern kingdom to earn herself a nickname like the Dame of Dust now, would it?"

"Uncle Citan, it's adorable how you still try to protect a warrior maiden such as myself. Understand that nothing will keep me from seeing a flabbergasted Grammy when she sees her people's sky-blue eyes radiating from your people's ebony skin. I do hope it's not too much for the old gal. If she does faint or something, I nominate you to give her mouth-to-mouth resuscitation."

* * *

Roe watched the Nominious soldiers lining up for battle. Glancing at the two hundred guards with him was disheartening.

"How many warriors does the Zuzax tribe have?" he asked Pomii.

"None. We aren't a warrior, people. We just hunt and farm and fish."

"Well, Yao should be arriving any minute now unless something happened, but let's try to stay positive," Roe said as he entered the largest structure in the village that served as both the meeting hall and Grammy's residence. As they crossed the hall towards the back room where the matriarch resided, they saw a strange glow coming from around the door. Upon entering, they saw Grammy sitting on a cushion, holding an oak box with several glowing runes. Upon opening the box, she removed a large conch shell that burned green.

"Tell everyone to get ready for a storm," Grammy said to her attendants, even though there wasn't a cloud in the sky.

"What is that thing?" Roe asked as they followed the matriarch outside and up the stairs to the roof of the meeting hall.

"That horn comes from a group of people who can breathe water and air. Legend has it that they live on the back of a giant sea serpent."

Roe's heart began to race as a smile eased onto his face with the memory of a green-illuminated serpent setting a hurricane on fire.

As the invading soldiers approached, Grammy put the horn to her lips and blew with all her might, but nothing happened. She tried this several times before finally handing it to Pomii as the soldiers began to set fire to the houses on the outskirts of the village. Pomii met with the same success as Grammy had.

Roe took the shell as the Zuzax people began screaming as they fled to the northern end of the village. Remembering the sound he had heard on Yaoite Island, he blew into the shell and met with the same results. Seconds later, almost like an echo, the shell sent out a deafening blast that shook everybody to their core. Instantly the skies darkened, and the wind whipped up to hurricane forces.

Without the protection of the caves, Roe watched as the village flew apart as he and Pomii helped Grammy climb down the steps. As they reached the ground, another horn blast was heard far out to sea. Roe strained his eyes and could just barely make out something green slithering through the dark storm clouds. Once inside, they noticed most of the village had already gathered.

"We will be safe from the storm here," Grammy said. "This building was built on the island's bedrock."

Roe grabbed a long rope before turning to his brother with a huge smile.

"I can't miss this," he said, heading for the door.

"Can't-miss what? Aren't you afraid of whatever is answering our call?"

"I am terrified; that's what's so exciting!" And with that, he disappeared into the storm.

Roe wedged himself between three tall trees before anchoring himself with the rope. He looked up, mesmerized as half of the sky slithered by as green flashes arced, and the earth shook as several horns bellowed. The sky twisted and turned as it dipped closer to the ground while green flashes leaped to earth. Roe watched through the swirling darkness as brief moments of green light struck the Nominious soldiers. After what felt like an eternity, the sky slithered back out to sea, and moments later, the storm clouds vanished.

CHAPTER 30

"You Southerners tend to bring your heads down over your food instead of sitting up straight and bringing the food to your mouth," Lilith said, enjoying a meal with her new friends. "I mean, I can understand why you do that; it's because you don't have long, gorgeous hair like some of us. Your loss."

"Well, my father used to have shoulder length—" Roe began.

"And how about when you drink, why do you Southerners raise your little finger? Maybe it affects the cup's contents, or maybe you just had your nails polished, and the little fingernail isn't dry. In that case, smelling the polish would affect your taste while you drink. I am sure that's a thing with you guys, but I think you would get a better sniff if you raised your pointer finger, but you would probably poke yourself in the eye if you did that."

Roe looked over at Pomii, who appeared to be dying as he silently shook while trying to keep his mouth shut as he ate.

"And what about spoons? Do you guys still set each table with spoons, or are they brought out only when you are served soup, which is the proper way one should do it. Otherwise, what's the point of a spoon?" Lilith asked. "And butter knives, why have I seen a fish knife used instead of a butter knife? They are very (cough), very (cough, cough) . . .

The guys watched as Lilith pulled at her collar and tried to get a drink. She began to claw frantically at her neck as her face turned purple. Leaping to her feet, she tried to move towards the doorway but spun in place just before collapsing.

Roe was the first to her side and noticed her eyes had rolled back in her head as white bubbles flowed from her mouth and nose. He placed her on her side, but her body became rigid as she began to convulse. He called out for help, and a guard rushed into the room and froze.

Pomii rushed past the guard with a purple leaf in his hand, and he instructed Roe to hold open her mouth as he crushed the leaf before placing it on her tongue. They watched as Lilith's breathing began normalizing and her body quit convulsing. No sooner had Pomii sat back in relief than the guard came over and delivered a savage kick to the side of his head. As he crumpled to the ground, the guard drew his short sword and pointed it at Roe.

"This isn't us; we didn't do anything to her," Roe said as the guard raised his blade. There was something about the angle of the strike that was all wrong. He placed both hands on the floor and kicked the guard as hard as possible in his midsection, knocking him backward. Roe jumped up, grabbed two steak knives, and lunged for the guard.

The guard had already regained his balance and swung for Roe's head. Blocking the sword with one knife, he stepped in closer and slid the other between his ribs. As the guard gasped, Roe dropped the first knife and wrenched the sword out of the guard's hand before pulling the second knife out of his side. Without hesitation, he inserted his short blade just above the collarbone and out the back of his neck.

"What do you think you are doing?" Lilith asked, looking first at where Pomii lay, then at the fallen guard as Roe stood over him with a bloody sword.

"This isn't what it looks like," Roe said as Pomii began to moan.

"You mean that you didn't kill that guard?" Lilith asked.

"No, I did kill the guard, but—"

"So it's exactly what it looks like, GUARDS!" Lilith yelled.

"If I may," Pomii said, getting to his feet. "How many guards do you have that are Southerners?"

"What? None. All of my guards come from the merchants guild…." Lilith began as she realized that the dead guard had pale skin. Roe knelt and removed the fake guard's helmet. After pulling down the collar of his jacket, he discovered a tattoo of a crown with an arrow piercing it.

"Look at this," he called to the others. "This is the tattoo of the king slayer, and the only person I know of who has this is the assassin Lefterry."

* * *

"So why do you go by Roe instead of Royce?" Lilith asked as the two of them sat in front of her hearth atop the fur of a rather large beast.

"It was a decision I made when I changed families. I cannot go back to the life I used to know because I killed a noble."

"From what I understand," Lilith said, scooting closer, "it was a thirteen-year-old boy defending himself against the attacks of a fully grown man."

"Well, the laws are rather firm on . . . " As Lilith's face almost touched his, Roe forgot what he was about to say. The smell of her hair, was that jasmine? It didn't matter, nothing else seemed to matter as her soft lips pressed against his, and he drank of her love.

"Guys!" Pomii said, barging into the room as Roe secretly wished he was an only child again. "Grammy just heard from some of the Zuzax people in the south. The castle is about to be seized by Houses Dular and Nominious! They have plans to eliminate the council of elders, along with your uncle."

Roe leaped to his feet and started for the door, but Lilith grabbed his hand.

"Do you want the help of my people?" she asked as her blue eyes bored into his. "Then take charge of my kingdom."

"What?" Roe said, pulling his hand away.

"If you want my help, I want you to fulfill me as a woman. I want you to take me as your wife and give me babies."

CHAPTER 31

The old general Zosi accompanied Ivan and the elders into the council chambers early that morning. After the doors were closed, the guards signaled each other, and as one man, they sealed the chamber. Knowing that they would be in there for several hours, it was doubtful they would even realize they were trapped until much later.

Each house contributed soldiers to serve in the royal army. Still, over the past two months, the rotation schedule had gradually arranged for soldiers belonging to House Dular and Nominious to guard the inner chambers. Soldiers from House Kastlet had been assigned to guard the castle on the remote outpost at the Belthane border. House Sovan soldiers had been assigned guard positions on the remote outpost near the Nominious border.

Arranging for securing the heads of state in the chamber was the easy part of the plan. The challenging part would be holding them there without discovery while the rest of their forces locked down the castle.

Ivan had called for his guards to consist of soldiers from House Sovan, but that message had never been delivered for some reason.

"We have been instructed to bring refreshments to the chamber at this hour," a blue-eyed server announced. Moments later, he returned to the kitchen with the refreshments still with him. Messengers were ordered to give their messages to the guards or to return whenever they opened the chamber doors.

While the guards were intent on keeping intruders out of the chamber, they slowly realized that nobody had ever tried to leave. Typically, there would be envoys between the houses, messengers with governances on the various aspects of the kingdom, and the need to take a break - none of which happened in the past five hours.

After a dozen Nominious and Dular soldiers arrived, the guards opened the side door to the chamber, and they streamed in. Once inside, they were greeted by a lone elder.

"Brothers, I have noticed that our messengers haven't arrived from either the Northern kingdom or the Kastlet lands," Elder Mattias said in hushed tones to the others gathered an hour after they had entered the chamber. Elder Johannes crept over to the nearest chamber door as silence descended on the room. After unsuccessfully attempting to open it, General Zosi turned to Ivan after withdrawing his sword.

"We knew it was only a matter of time before this happened." In a louder voice, he addressed the room. "Ladies, gentlemen, and esteemed elders, in light of our current situation, I hereby initiate Operation Living Legend. Godspeed to us all."

Wordlessly, Elder Lucas went over to the bookshelf and withdrew three books before pressing the stones behind them. As he did, the hearth slid to one side, as did the conference table and a large portrait of the first-ever sovereign of the island, revealing three passages. When General Zosi attempted to accompany Ivan past the portrait and into the passage behind it, the regent held him back.

"My safety is not important. I need you to get back to Sovan and guard our estate."

"I am sorry, Regent Ivan, but I cannot do that," General Zosi said. "Under the articles of the operation, the priority of the highest-ranking official present is the security of the sovereign."

Looking at the old general and then over at Elder Lucas, Ivan hesitated.

"Go on, get out of here. We all know why I was selected to stay behind," the elder said as he sealed up the other two passages. After further prompting from Zosi, Ivan hurried through the passage and into the darkness.

Upon speaking the word 'Illuminati,' small orbs of light glowed into existence along the winding corridor. The passageway led a tremendous distance before turning a corner into a dead end. While everybody searched for the hidden switch, the orbs suddenly swayed in the air.

"Someone has entered this passage," the old general said.

"Lucas would never betray us; it's not like he can feel pain or anything," Ivan said, tapping on another stone.

With the sound of footsteps hurrying down the passage, Zosi positioned himself between Ivan and the newcomer. Moments later, Elder Lucas appeared.

"Seeing as the elders are the only ones who know about the secret levers to open the passages, I thought you might need a hand."

The back wall slid open as the elder pressed a completely circular stone embedded into the wall while standing on an identical one. The blue-eyed kitchen staff froze as one of the walls slid away to reveal the group from the chambers.

"We thought we would save you the trouble of bringing us lunch," Zosi said with a wink.

"What's going on?" one of the cooks asked. "Why are there soldiers surrounding the kitchen? Are we under attack?"

Hurrying to the window, Zosi looked at a squad of soldiers from House Dular.

"Where do you keep your kitchen clothes?" Ivan asked the cook.

Sometime later, two people wearing cook's clothes walked past the guards as they carried out the trash. Several minutes later, a group left carrying food to one of the castle wings.

Once outside of the castle, Ivan and Zosi entered the stables of an inn owned by House Belthane. As they changed into the clothes lent to them by the Zuzax cooks, they failed to notice three Kastlet guards watching them.

"What do we have here, boys?" the first one said, walking forward. "Slaves without blue eyes."

"Unless I miss my guess, this here is General Zosi and the regent whose blood Count Christoff swore would stain his sword," said the second one as they drew their blades.

As Zosi leaped towards the nearest two soldiers, Ivan grabbed a pitchfork to defend himself against the third. The first soldier dodged the general's attack and joined the third one in attacking Ivan. When

Zosi hurried to stand beside Ivan, he underestimated his opponent's speed, and his blade penetrated the old general's heart.

The second soldier turned in shock to look at the general as Ivan pierced his head with the pitchfork. Grabbing his fallen sword, he dispatched the third soldier, who struggled to free his blade from the general's chest. Doing so exposed himself to the blade of the last soldier and left Ivan with a sharp pain in his side. He doubled over as the guard came to deliver a fatal blow, but suddenly he stood and thrust his blade through the guard's neck before he himself collapsed.

CHAPTER 32

"Since Nominious soldiers are attacking the capitol, they probably wouldn't take kindly to our march across their lands in our journey to attack them," Citan said as he studied a map of the Southern kingdom alongside Maxwell and Roe. At the same time, Lilith oversaw the preparations to depart.

"We would have to journey there through the Belthane lands," Roe added to the laughter of the two brothers.

"The House Belthane hates us more than any other house because of the death of their beloved prince," Maxwell began.

"Well, not to rule out House Kastlet. They are begrudging us for interrupting their fishing lanes with our merchant ships," Citan added.

"That would mean the three hundred and fifty some odd merchant guards, combined with the Sovan family soldiers versus the entire Southern kingdom," Roe said, summing up the situation.

"I am going to check on how Lilith is doing with the preparations," Maxwell said, nodding to his brother.

"Roe, when are you going to step up and take on the responsibilities of House Sovan? I get it, your past isn't perfect, but nobodies is," Citan said.

"That chapter of my life is closed for me. Now I am just going to live as a Yaoite."

"Roe, that's a coward's choice, and if you are going to run from your responsibilities as the eldest son of your house, you have no business with Lilith. She doesn't need a boy running around playing soldier while avoiding real responsibilities. She needs a man who knows his place and fights the hard fight that comes with standing up for his family."

* * *

The journey to Celestia took the entire day. That evening when all the ships were loaded, Maxell and Lilith joined Citan at the local tavern.

"Where's Roe? Did either of you scare him off because, during the entire trip up here and loading everything up, he hasn't even said two words to me," Lilith said.

"Well, I am sure there is a lot on his mind. He is going home for the first time in five years," Citan replied.

"He needs to know that I am here for him and that I love him."

"Lilith, I think he knows," Maxwell said gently. "There are just some things a man has to do on his own. Now we need to get some sleep. We had a long ride and will be in Sovan lands tomorrow."

Upon overhearing this, the man sitting next to them tossed a few coins on the table and left. He slowly walked towards the deepest shadow in the alley that joined the tavern and waited. Moments later, another man ducked down the same alley.

"It's just as you suspected, Clyde," the newcomer said. "From what I overheard from the merchant guards, they just got back from a fight before riding up here."

"And now they are getting ready for another one," Clyde said.

"So what's the plan?"

"We get our guys together as we wait for them to nod off. With all the fighting and riding they have done, sleep should come easy to these guys," Clyde said. "Way I see it, they have just gifted us with all the weapons we need to take their castle from them, and from my count, we won't get much resistance."

"This is going to be great. Not only will they get wiped out in the battle, but those who survive also won't have a home to return to."

The two men were soon joined by two more as they made their way down toward the waters. After a quick discussion, they decided which boat held the most weapons and supplies and began climbing up the sides. It was mildly surprising that there were no guards on duty, and after a quick inspection of the bunks, the crew was nowhere in sight. Upon reaching the cargo hold, they quickly realized they were not alone.

* * *

As the sun rose over the waters, the Northerners made two discoveries: a group of men tied up on the docks, and their ships were blocked in by ships with black sails with red crosses. Roe almost leaped with excitement as the first one docked, and Yao strode off. Running up to him, Roe stopped short, seeing the look on his face.

"Roe, I have questions of you, and you will give answers to me."

While the others moved to join them, Citan held them back.

"Yao I—"

"SILENCE! I took you in; I trained you and provided for you. Why have you betrayed your oath to me?"

"Yao, I don't understand what you mean by this. My loyalty remains to you. I joined myself to the Zuzax to fulfill my duties to you," Roe said, looking over at the Yaoite ships and the two warriors he had sent to report back to Yao.

"Roe, what have you done with my son? Where is June?"

Roe's eyes widened as he slowly began to see the family resemblance. As the color crept into his face, all he could do was hang his head.

"You will accompany me to his burial place. As you know, we have a duty never to leave our people behind," Yao said.

As he stood there, a change came over him. Roe's features relaxed as he raised his head, meeting Yao's gaze.

"Your son was killed in a cowardly attack by House Nominious. You have taught me early on that a person's duty lies to his people and his family. I have a duty I must fulfill to my family because I am Royce, the first son of Leotan Sovan. You have a duty to House Sovan, and you are honor bound to fulfill that duty as Yao of the Yaoites. Before all gather here today, I charge you to aid us in opposing our common enemy. June's body will remain undisturbed until order has been restored. Now is not the time to remember our dead; now is the time to exact revenge on our enemies."

CHAPTER 33

Ivan grimaced, partly from the wound in his side and partly from seeing a member of House Belthane whipping a Zuzax man.

"Does this displease you, Ivan?" asked Reginald, the current Bastion of Belthane. "I cannot imagine how you motivate the Zuzaxes to get anything done."

"We have found out that money is a good motivator," Ivan replied with a wince.

"But they are savages, Ivan."

"And you know that I believe all men are created equal."

"And for all of your fine ideas and virtue signaling, here we are," Reginald said as he held up a glass of red wine and gauged its transparency.

"It's not virtue signaling to oppose oppression and the wrong done to others, Reginald."

"Isn't it, though? Why flaunt it if you aren't trying to appear better than everybody else?"

"I treat the Zuzax people respectfully because that is the right thing to do, just as righting the wrongs done to House Kastlet is the right thing to do," Ivan said.

"Careful, Ivan, it almost sounded like you think of these savages as equals to one of our five great houses. Why did they allow us to enslave them if we are all so equal? No, my dear brother-in-law, we are not all equals, for if they could stand up to us, they would, but because they cannot, it just proves that we are their superiors."

"And what should you do if House Dular and Nominious should turn on you and make you their slaves?" Ivan asked.

"Preposterous!"

"I would wager that House Kastlet would have said the same thing a few months ago," Ivan said. "Why would either house need to pay for your crops if all they needed was to do away with the seller? There would be no expense lost on the laborers; they work for free."

Ivan watched the tips of Reginald's ears turn pink as he pretended to study his wine.

"You know, they have reached out to me. At least Ashwind has; I haven't heard anything from Brassmas," Reginald said, setting his glass down on the table and finally giving Ivan his full attention.

"One simply cannot overlook what they did to Christoff. If we did that, we would be no better than those savages."

"Then join me in opposing the wrong done to a royal house. Not only have they all but destroyed a house, they have attacked a reigning regent. What law do you believe that they hold precious?" Ivan said, pressing a hand to his wound that had opened again.

"Ashwind promised me your lands if I would join him and House Nominious," Reginald said.

"And what would that gain you? My lands aren't as fertile as yours. What would a feud between our houses accomplish but deplete our forces so that we will be easier to conquer by our enemies?"

"I will join your cause, my dear brother-in-law, but I have my conditions," Reginald said, finishing his wine.

"And pray tell what those maybe?"

"I think we agree that Brassmas and Ashwind must be held accountable for their crimes. This is no small condition, though. Never before has a member of a ruling house been condemned; we have always held ourselves above such things as laws and rules."

"Agreed," Ivan said.

"There is a second matter that we need to come to an understanding on," Reginald said, pouring himself another glass of wine. Holding it up to the sun, he commented about the excellencies of the summer blend.

"Are you referring to the matter of a sovereign?" Ivan asked.

"Precisely. With all the turmoil and recovery that needs to occur, I would like your house to withdraw from the Contest of Kings."

"Reginald, you cannot be serious! With Ashwind and Brassmas denounced and Christoff living on an island somewhere, you would want me to withdraw so you could become sovereign unopposed? And why is that? Do you feel this is the only way you could gain supremacy if everyone else withdraws?"

"My dear Ivan, just look at yourself. You are falling apart. You served as regent for five years, and your time as sovereign regent has not been kind to you. As the strongest candidate for House Sovan, you are a mere shadow of your former self. You need to rest and recover, not push yourself until you collapse. What good will you do the kingdom if we need to find another sovereign one year after your ascension?"

"Very well, if that's what it takes to return peace to the kingdom, then I will do as you ask," Ivan said with a sigh.

"As the future sovereign of our kingdoms, I commit to you my support," Reginald said with a smile.

"My summer home is bigger than this palace," Brassmas said, standing in the ruins that formally housed the Count of Kastlet.

"But it does have its strategic advantages," Ashwind said as he picked his way over the rubble and over to where Brassmas stood, looking out a large bay window towards the high castle in the northeast.

"Yes. This 'palace' is the closest stronghold to the high castle, an odd place for land that makes its living off fishing. With a garrison of our troops stationed here, none will be able to challenge our sovereignty."

"Speaking of troops, how many are left after that debacle in the north?" Ashwind asked.

"That was an unforeseen disaster. How could anyone plan for the ancient sea creature coming to the aid of the Zuzax or for the presence of something called 'thunder worms?'"

"You do it by careful planning and consideration of all of your variables. For instance, had your troops taken an extra day to go around the valley pass—"

"As I recall, your infamous marauders didn't fare so well either," Brassmas said.

"And if you would also recall, my army did just successfully defeat the Yaoites on their island."

"I do recall that just like I also recall that they were still recovering from an attack by the Sardinians."

"And I suppose that the people of Sardis just happened to attack the Yaoites just before my troops arrived? Those same Sardanas whom we happen to have healthy trade relations with?" Ashwind asked.

The two stood watching their laborers repair the palace for several minutes of silence.

"How did it go with Reginald?" Brassmas finally asked.

"I don't believe he will work with us but don't worry. If things continue to go as I suspect, he will serve our needs as our enemy's enemy."

CHAPTER 34

Royce stood alone on the pier that led to the Sovan palace as he watched a lady hurrying towards him. He tried to step towards her, but his legs wouldn't cooperate. Holding on to anything he could find for support, all he could do was wait until she arrived. Moments later, he collapsed, sobbing in his mother's arms.

"How long has it been, Lynn?" Lady Ellen asked her sister.

"Five years, eight months, and three days since I last saw my boy," Lynn said as she watched Royce directing the unloading of the ships.

"But why did he have to bring merchants with him? Especially those merchants."

"That's enough out of you, Ellen. Any friend of Royce's is welcome here."

While Lynn left her sister to oversee the accommodations of her guests, the Zuzax workers brought the last of the cargo into the storage barn.

"You, boy, that doesn't go in there. That shed is for dry goods. Runner beast supplies go in the barn," Ellen said

Pomii stared at Lady Ellen for several minutes. He had never seen someone so richly dressed before.

"Did you hear what I said? Runner mounts. Barn. Understand? I swear Lynn's approach to the Zuzax is unacceptable. Her workers must be some of the slowest people I have ever met," she said as she hurried to join her sister.

She hadn't gone more than five steps before she collided with a dark-skinned, blue-eyed young lady.

"Excuse me, but in this house, it is customary for the guests to stay in the guest quarters, not run through the halls like they belong here."

"My apologies; I didn't realize this was your house," Lilith said.

"My name is Lady Ellen Belthane, and I am the sister of Lady Lynn Sovan. You would do well to remember that while you are here."

"Oh, so you are a guest here as well! Excellent. You may show me to the guest quarters, and please ensure I get the largest one as is fitting."

"*Excuse me!?*" Ellen said.

"You are excused. And seeing as you are just a lady and I am an empress, you would do well to remember your manners in my presence. It's the least you can do."

"Just who do you think you are?" Ellen shouted.

"You mean you don't know? Because I definitely remember you, Ellen of Belthane," she said, drawing closer to Ellen.

"My name is Lilith, and I am the empress of the entire Northern kingdom."

"The cursed princess!"

"Does hardness of hearing accompany that ridiculous hairstyle of yours? I clearly said my title was *empress.* I inherited that title from my late father; you remember him, the guy you were flirting with after your second bottle of wine."

"Why, you filthy little half-breed. If you were in my lands, I would have you whipped for talking to me like that."

"Lady Ellen," Royce said, entering the hallway ahead of his mother. "I will not abide you or anyone speaking to the lady I will make my wife with such disrespect. Are we clear?"

"Lynn, I am sorry, I cannot stay here a minute longer," Ellen said just before rushing outside and screaming for her coach.

"Of course, you have every right to blame Ivan Sovan, he was the regent at the time, and while Brassmas and Ashwind bear the majority of the blame, ultimately, it is the responsibility of the sovereign to intervene when two monarchs violate the rule of law.

Something I assure you, my dear Christoff, that I would have acted on swiftly."

Reginald sat in his usual chair on the upper open balcony overlooking the Zuzax, hard at work in his vineyards. Across from him sat a rather haggard-looking Count Christoff alongside an untouched glass of wine. The count and his few remaining staff had been granted sanctuary on the Belthane plantation.

"I appreciate all you have done for us and realize that this may put you in a difficult position with your neighbors to the south."

"Family affairs are challenging indeed. With my marriage to your sister and my sister's marriage to the Sovans, well, nothing is simple, is it?"

"Reginald, Reginald, I have just been attacked while visiting our sister!" Ellen said, barging in on the conversation, slightly out of breath. "That evil witch who caused the death of your son is now living with the Sovans."

"Ellen, my dear, please calm yourself and tell me what you are going on about," Reginald asked.

Ellen related how she had been assaulted by a young girl who demanded that she give up her quarters to appease some self-imposed claims she had to royalty. Before she learned her identity, she had been insulted by the recently returned Royce.

"And you are sure that Royce said that he is going to marry her?"

"I am not a moron, Reginald. I heard what he said, and I assure you I will not lose another nephew to that evil thing."

"Well, this changes things," Reginald said. "I wonder why Ivan didn't mention this when he was here yesterday?"

"Ivan was here?" Christoff said, jumping to his feet. "Asking for your help, I presume?"

"Calm yourself, my dear brother-in-law. We made no deal between us. He just came here to get a feel for where I stand on things, but if he is harboring that wretch who killed my son and didn't tell me about it, well, Ivan Sovan is no friend of this house."

Christoff took his seat and picked up his wine glass as he watched a storm beginning out at sea.

"They did it to themselves, you know," he said, taking a sip. "Ignoring our plight while aligning themselves with your enemies, House Sovan has sealed their fate."

CHAPTER 35

“Watch,” Brassmas said as he petted a most unusual hairless creature with a long tail that came up to about his knees. He motioned to a man with pale skin and black curly hair who took the silver whistle from around his neck and blew a sharp note. Instantly the creature rushed forward into the open field along with several other hairless creatures. After a command, they stopped, and a thick purple cloud covered the entire field.

“When I learned that two battalions had been lost to some strange animal, I remembered hearing a story about an unusual pet they cultivated in Ashmerria, a small country in the mainland. I reached out to some of my friends in Ashmerria, and they agreed to lend them to me for our upcoming defeat of the Sovans.”

“Hmm, I see. So these hairless ones can cover the entire battlefield with a thick cloud, so they won’t see us coming? Couldn’t we wait until night and achieve the same effect?” Ashwind asked.

With a nod from Brassmas, the Ashmerrian sounded another note on his whistle. There was a quick flash, and with a roar, the entire field erupted into a sea of boiling fire. A few minutes later, the fires had subsided, and the creatures came running back to their handlers.

“Well, that explains their hairlessness,” Ashwind said. “In other news, I heard from Reginald. While he made it clear, as I told you, that he isn’t interested in supporting our cause directly, he will be taking personal actions against his neighbor.”

"So it would appear that your hunch on the matter has paid off," Brassmas said. "Did he happen to mention what his plans were so we may be able to coordinate?"

"While he wasn't very forthcoming, I was able to gather from my men who are spying on him that by tomorrow, there should either be a Belthane flag flying over their palatial mansions or it will be burned to the ground."

"I wonder what Ivan did to anger them so much. No matter, we have before us the small matter of securing the capitol from the royal army, but with the numbers, we have on our side and these magnificent fire cats, I don't see them being much of a problem," Brassmas said, turning to mount his runner beast.

"There are a couple of items to note," Ashwind said, stopping his friend. "On the one hand, the Kastlets have joined the Belthanes against the Sovans. On the other hand, Ivan seems to have acquired some new friends. It would appear that the merchant guards from the Northern kingdom have joined him but not to worry. My sources say they only add about three hundred guards to his troops, and we both know that a guard is no soldier."

Coughing, Ivan pushed himself up on his bed as Royce entered.

"Come in, my boy. You have grown from a lad to a man! Let me have a look at you."

Royce noticed the dark blood oozing from his uncle's side, and his face fell.

"No, no, there is no time for that. I have lived a good life, and now it is time for me to pass the torch, so to speak."

"There is still time for you to recover. We have some of the best healers—"

"No," Ivan said as another spasm of coughing shook him. "The soldier's blade was true to its mark. I will be gone before the sun sets."

"I never had the chance to thank you for saving my life all those years ago," Royce began before Ivan held up a weak hand.

"If you want to honor me truly, then you must listen closely."

Ivan struggled to sit up with Royce's help.

"Always defend the rights of those who cannot stand up for themselves. Never betray a trust, even if it costs you. Only rule on a matter once you have personally and thoroughly searched out the matter for yourself. Put strong drink far from you, and lastly, learn to listen to everything as if your life depends on it because it does."

With that, Ivan gave a final cough and was gone.

* * *

Later that night, as dirt was packed into the hole over Ivan's coffin, the family quietly made their way back to the palace.

"This is a terrible sign," Pomii whispered to his cousin.

"I agree. The death of a patriarch on the eve of battle bodes ill for us, but Roe, or Royce as we now should be calling him, doesn't need to hear anything from us but encouragement," Lilith said.

The following morning as the sun rose over the Sovan army, they began their long march toward the castle. When they had reached the boundaries of the palace, Pomii rode up to Royce.

"I have searched everywhere and cannot find any sign of them. Yao and his Yaoites have completely abandoned us."

Chapter 36

"How long have you known Royce?" Lady Lynn asked Lilith as they stocked medical supplies into a palace wing converted for that purpose.

"We have known each other for over a week," Lilith answered.

"And you decided he is the one you'll marry in that short time?"

"If you ask me, she should forget about marriage and focus on her kingdom. There will be time for that other stuff later," Cinthia said as she stacked vials containing salve in a wall compartment next to the clean towels that Lynn was stocking.

"I don't think that's a very good idea," Lilith said quietly as she handed Lynn another set of towels.

"*Oh!?*" Cinthia said.

"My aunt Liz served as head of the merchants guild for ten years before suddenly quitting one day because she wanted to raise a family. She has found more satisfaction and meaning in her life as a wife and a mother than she ever did running the guild."

"That's just one person, child," Cinthia said. "You cannot base your life on how someone else lives theirs."

"Well, my uncle Maxwell's wife, Jenny, managed all of his record books for years, but after a big fight, he does all of the books, and she raises my cousin Jasper. And everybody who knows them agrees that they are much happier now."

"It may be possible that a woman finds fulfillment both in business and in being a wife and mother," Lynn said

"I don't know about that," Lilith said. "The time a woman wastes running things takes away from the crucial things in life, like a family.

"Maybe you people are different, though," she continued. "Maybe you are happy involving yourself working on stuff instead of raising your own kids and caring for the man who loves you. I don't know how you can have a family and leave them to raise themselves. It's not somebody else's family; it's yours."

"It's clear you are an incredibly naïve little girl who refuses to listen to the advice of her elders," Cinthia said before moving away.

"My aunt Liz never wanted to get married, and she never wanted the burden of raising kids, but after she quit the guild and married, she told me that she felt like she had been robbed of the past ten years of her life."

"What Miss Cinthia means is that you shouldn't base your life on one person's advice," Lynn offered.

"Do you disagree with me?" Lilith asked. "Which means more to you, running this estate or your son?"

"Well, Royce, of course."

"And my children will mean more to me than any old job as an empress could. And as far as what Miss Cinthia was saying, I think she is saying those things out of the hurt she feels for June, but I think it would be better to love and be hurt than never to love at all because you are too busy running things."

"We will wait here," Royce said, halting his army in a grove of trees that bordered the high castle.

"We need to scout the area and find out how many we are going up against and where their troops lie," Citan said.

"Pomii," Royce called. "I need you to contact the Zuzax in the castle and learn as much as possible about the Nominious and Dular armies. Go to the north side; that's where the servants' quarters are."

Pomii rode his runner beast to the north, utilizing as much tree line as possible. Coming upon a group gathering wood for the kitchen, he dismounted and introduced himself. The other Zuzax quickly had him change clothes as they rushed him to the palace.

"You need to rescue Elder Lucas," the man who had identified himself as Ameelee said.

"Brother, I am not here on a rescue mission. I need to find out how many people we are going against," Pomii said.

"If you want our help, you must help the elder first. He has been very kind to our people."

As Ameelee led Pomii deeper into the castle, Pomii quickly lost his way. As they drew closer to the dungeon, memories of another dungeon caused him to pull back. Ameelee looked at him for a moment before assuring him he was safe. The two came to a prison cell where the elder was suspended by one arm. The other was lying on a table nearby where it had been twisted off. Ameelee produced a key and freed the elder.

"If you already had the key, why do you need me?" Pomii asked.

"You are carrying a sword; I assume you know how to use it. We are forbidden from arming ourselves."

As the two gently freed the elder, he rushed past them and into the hallway as the guards returned. Turning a lampstand while pressing a blue and grey stone, a panel popped open, and the three slid inside. Little orbs of light appeared when the elder spoke "Illuminati" into the darkness as Pomii began to tend to the elder's arm.

"What do you make of that?" the first guard to arrive back in the dungeon asked. He stood alongside the lampstand and regarded a wall section that emanated a faint glow.

"Seems to me we have a bigger problem here," the other guard said, indicating the empty chains.

"I see a connection," the first guard said, grabbing a large hammer.

"Don't fuss about the arm; it's gone," Lucas said, hurrying down the corridor.

"Elder, what we need—" Pomii began.

"What you need is to be quiet and follow me. You have a sword, meaning you are from the north. If you are from the north, that must mean the only house the Zuzax have any loyalty to has asked for their help. These passages lead throughout the castle, and only the elders know how to access them."

A loud crash behind them caused them all to race forward. The elder stopped before a wall and compressed a series of stones. As the panel gave way, he uttered the word "un-Illuminati," and the passageway grew dark.

"This room should allow you a great view to the west where there is—" Lucas began before realizing that he had just walked them into a room full of soldiers.

"There's the signal," Ashwind said as he looked through his field glass toward the Sovan's land.

"Then Reginald and Christoff are on their way," Brassmas added.

"I don't believe they have encountered the Sovans yet, so that must mean they are already here," Ashwind said, placing his glass back in its case.

"All right, listen up," Brassmas said to the attending commanders. "I want a fire cat issued to every patrol. When you see the Sovans, release the cats and let them do their job. If you see fire, send your cats in that direction. Let them initiate the battle and then proceed to destroy the rest."

Brassmas and Ashwind watched the tree line to the castle's east as several fires erupted among them. As their soldiers lined up between the castle and the forest, their archers unleashed a volley of arrows into the trees.

"Ready the lancers on the runner beasts," Ashwind commanded.

"Those merchants' guards are worthless in a fight," Brassmas said, laughing as he held up his field glass.

Ashwind looked to where Brassmas was indicating and let out a short laugh.

"Maybe nobody told them what to do in an actual battle."

In the forest, the guards hadn't even pulled their swords from their sheaths. Instead, Citan was leading them in placing their hands around their mouths and making bird calls. A while later, the guards repeated the call as several birds arrived.

The fire cats were captivated by the birds to such an extent that they ignored their handlers' commands. Regardless, every movement they made generated more of the deadly purple mist. The entire forest was now shrouded in the fog as more and more birds arrived.

"Retreat, retreat!" Ashwind called, running for the castle.

"Ashwind, get back here. We have them exactly where we want them," Brassmas yelled in vain as the Dular soldiers began withdrawing from the battle.

Moments later, Brassmas realized that with the arrival of the birds, the winds had also changed.

"Give the command to ignite the gas, you idiots!" Brassmas commanded the nearest Ashmerrian.

"It's no good, sir. They won't respond to us," the man said as the deadly purple mist was blown from the forest and across the soldiers standing on the open field. Brassmas had just made out the white teeth of a large smile on the man leading the guards as he struck two stones together, causing a spark that incinerated most of the standing army and caught the castle on fire.

"Well, that was fun," Citan said, checking on Royce as the birds flew away.

"We need to press every advantage we get," he said as a messenger rode up from the east.

"Royce, I have a message for you from your mom. She says the Belthanes and Kastlets are on their way here after destroying your home. She, Lilith, and Cinthia are fine, though, after escaping with the help of the Zuzax."

Chapter 37

The palace guard heard a scraping sound, looked over the edge of the balcony, and discovered four men climbing up the side walls just before an arrow penetrated his head. The second guard saw him drop and went to investigate as a hand reached up the banister. The guard froze as a man clad in all black pulled himself over and stared at him. Grabbing his horn, the guard sounded an alarm before drawing his sword. The black-clad man cut him down with two strikes before helping men dressed in similar attire over the balcony.

Moments later, five guards rushed to the balcony. A Zuzax serving lady bowed as they went by and, after making sure that no more guards were approaching, motioned to more of the black-clad assassins who were concealing themselves in the large room connected to the balcony. While the guards confronted the assassins leaning on the banister, the other assassins attacked the guards from behind and cut them down.

"That's most of the ones guarding the house. There are several more guarding the roads, but they won't come here unless ordered," the Zuzax woman said.

"Those have already been dealt with; now, direct us to where the family stays," said the unarmed assassin in charge.

While the Zuzax woman led him through the palace, she was pleased to notice the other Zuzax people had stopped working and began to follow her. Looking back, she was surprised that the other assassins had vanished. She was alone with the leader. Making her way into the study, Lady Nominious rose and demanded to know why the guards had sounded the alarm. Looking over her shoulder, the Zuzax woman realized that the assassin was nowhere to be seen.

"The sound came from the balcony on the second level. If you want to learn why the alarm was sounded, I suggest you make your way there," she said to the gasps of everybody gathered.

Lady Nominious quickly strode across the room and slapped the Zuzax woman.

"I am Lady Nominious—" she began before the Zuzax woman swung her fist, knocking the lady to the floor.

"Lady Nominious, you have given your last order to me or any other Zuzax person."

As the others jumped to their feet to support the lady of the house, they found their way was blocked by the other Zuzax in the room. Realizing they were outnumbered, the lady signaled a concealed corner of the room, and two bodyguards appeared.

Before they could take more than a step, the leader of the assassins suddenly appeared, and seconds later, both bodyguards lay at his feet.

"Lady Nominious," the Zuzax woman said. "You will accompany us now."

The Nominious family followed the Zuzax to a part of the palace grounds they had never been to before. Upon entering the dungeons, the Yaoites roughly shoved them into a cell where the rest of their family was waiting.

"Just in case it's unclear to you, the Zuzax people declare their liberty."

"Pomii," Royce called as he, along with the merchant guards and Sovans, battled through the remaining soldiers. Most consisted of the Dulars who had escaped the inferno in the front yard when Ashwind had commanded a retreat.

"Are you trying to find the Zuzax from the north?" a maid asked after tossing a bucket of water on the fire.

"Yes, his name is Pomii, and I am his brother," Royce said, showing the maid his star scar.

"The soldiers are holding him on the fifth floor along with one of the elders," she said as Royce and Citan raced towards the stairwell.

Bursting in on the guards' quarters, the first thing Royce noticed was the curved knife Ashwind held to Pomii's throat. The second thing he noticed was that he and Citan were outnumbered by twenty soldiers who pointed their weapons at them.

"Well, I guess this slave is important to you," Ashwind said.

To his surprise, Royce simply pulled out a chair and sat down after setting his sword on the table. The nearest soldier quickly removed it from arm's reach as Royce smiled at the Duke of Dular.

"You have caused us quite enough trouble with this little rebellion of yours," Ashwind said, removing the knife from Pomii's throat and shoving him toward the nearest soldier.

As he pulled out a chair and sat across from Royce, five soldiers in the back of the room collapsed.

"Ironically, Brassmas' little pets were the cause of his death, but that saves me the trouble of killing him later and making it look like an accident. Only one head may wear the crown here."

"Oh, he's not dead," Royce said. "His injuries prevent him from continuing this fight, but I have instructed my soldiers to take care of him as an enemy combatant who can no longer fight."

"And just what do you hope to gain by this? You have already lost. Right now, the combined might of both the Belthane and Kastlet forces are marching this way," Ashwind said as three more soldiers silently fell to the ground in the back of the room.

"And just whose side do you think the Kastlets will take? Uncle Ivan is dead, so now their only motivation is the death of you and Brassmas. It's obvious that they already have the support of the Belthanes."

"What's this?" Ashwind said, finally noticing the slain soldiers.

The remaining soldiers tried to turn but were killed where they stood as five men strode to the center of the room.

"Ashwind, Duke of Dular, meet Yao of the Yaoites. I assume you've heard of him."

Ashwind drew his dagger and lunged for Royce. Royce sprang up from his seat and barely managed to avoid the dagger's tip as it tore through his neck guard. Grabbing his wrist, Royce struck the inside of Ashwind's elbow, plunging the dagger into his heart.

"You have taken the revenge I am owed, Royce of the Sovans," Yao said.

"Royce Sovan, you are charged with the crime of killing the Noble of Nominious and the Duke of Dular. How do you respond to these charges?" Elder Mattias asked.

The throne room was noticeably empty, with the exception of the elders.

"I acted in self-defense in each case."

"So you say," Brassmas whispered from the chair, where he barely managed to hold himself up.

"Can you provide evidence of these claims?" asked Elder Johannes.

"I was alone when I encountered the Noble of Nominious, but as to my battle with the Duke of Dular, Yao was there to witness the battle."

Royce took his seat as Yao was called forth.

"It is as Royce has said, Ashwind lunged for him, and he defended himself."

"Objection," Brassmas whispered hoarsely. "Honorable elders, Yao's view of the situation should not be trusted because Ashwind had his forces attack Yaoite Island not too long ago. I submit that Yao may have a personal reason for siding against Ashwind."

"It was a fair fight, I say," Yao bellowed as the clerk called for order. "And if a leader of the House of Nominious cannot hold his own against a thirteen-year-old untrained boy, what soft leadership your house truly has."

While Yao took his seat and the clamor died down, Royce stood, walked over to the abandoned throne, and took a seat. While all gathered expressed their outrage, none dared move against him with the Yaoites present.

"Esteemed elders and representatives of households, my solution is rather simple. As of this day, I am abolishing the rights of the Sovans to own property outside of their family palace," Royce said. A wave of murmurs spread throughout the hall.

"Furthermore, I require each and every house to follow my lead and relinquish their lands for the commonwealth of all."

While outrage swept through the throne room, Royce waited for the clerk to regain order before proceeding.

"Furthermore, I am declaring the Zuzax people free with equal rights to every other person on the Island of the Mighty, and the houses that have unjustly inflicted servitude without compensation shall be required to make restitution for the grievances."

"Royce, you have lost your mind. Nobody will support you in this," Brassmas wheezed.

"Is that so?" Royce asked. "Tell me, Brassmas, do you currently know where your family is? Has anybody here wondered why their summons to their homelands have been unanswered and this throne room unfilled?"

"I will tell you why. It's because the Zuzax people have welcomed the Yaoites into their homes with open arms and now hold your entire families in your dungeons that I alone can grant release to," Royce said, holding up a ring of keys. "They will be released only after restitution has been made, or else I will personally ensure their exile from this island."

"You have ensured that the Zuzax oversee every little detail of your lives. Tell me, how much destruction do you think they can cause with the help of the deadliest fighters on the island? According to the last census, every ruling family member had an average of twelve slaves. That would make my blood brothers the largest population on this island."

After the court had adjourned, Royce and Citan watched in amusement as the heads of families tried to steer their carriages for the first time.

"Do you have the keys to all the dungeons?" Citan asked.

"I never said I did, but I did make my point, and people should learn not to judge on appearances."

CHAPTER 38

Grammy steadied herself as the boat approached Valvatine Island. Royce, Lilith, Pomii, Citan, Maxwell, Yao, Cinthia, and Lady Lynn were with her. As the boat eased onto a barge, Royce and Yao were the first to step out on the sand as the gentle breeze began picking up speed. Dark clouds began to blot out the sun but only over Valvatine Island. As dozens of other boats started to arrive from House Belthane, Sovan, Dular, and Nominious, a storm erupted as every dog and doglike creature began to howl.

"SILENCE," Grammy commanded, and the wind and rain eased off to a gentle patter.

"This is a fine day for our marriage, what? Was the cemetery not available?" Lilith said as she moved her soaked hair from her eyes.

"It must be this way to restore order to our fractured lands. If stability isn't established at the island's core, the lands will forever be in turmoil," Royce said.

"The chest with my dress had better still be dry; that's all I ask," Lilith said, casting a skeptical eye toward four Zuzax carrying a large chest between them. "Let's hurry out of the rain and inside, where ghosts, ghouls, creatures, and the undead are waiting. After all, we wouldn't want them to miss out on the opportunity to show their fealty now, would we?"

Ignoring her, Royce stepped in front of her and drew his sword as flashes of lightning revealed translucent man-wolf creatures directly in Grammy's path.

"Put that away," Grammy commanded without turning back. "These creatures would only destroy themselves if they moved against us. Master your fears; we must break the curse."

"Come on," Royce said to the newly appointed bastion, duke, and noble. "Surely you can at least match the courage of an old lady now, can't you?"

While they walked on through the half-light, the man-wolf creatures moved into the walls of the high castles. The procession couldn't help but stare as the shadows growled at them and watched them back with glowing red eyes. At the head of the procession, Grammy came to a chained gate leading to a massive courtyard where seven identical statutes faced each other on either side of the path. Grammy folded her hands and bowed her head in silence as a ray of sunlight pierced through the clouds. Seconds later, the chains fell off the gates, which swung open without help from a human hand.

While the procession moved across the courtyard, the sunbeam grew in intensity, causing a cleansing effect to wash over the ancient stones. Plants and overgrowth melted away to reveal ornate carvings, fountains, and statutes of animals long forgotten. The vines covering great wooden doors receded as the procession approached. The doors swung open in invitation as sunlight streamed into the once-dark halls.

"This way," Grammy said in hushed, reverent tones. Her staff seemed to retain the sunlight, and as she proceeded forward, the air would shimmer as the stones picked up on the light of her staff and reflected it, illuminating the long dark halls. Grammy continued to push back the darkness until she stood at the head of the great room. Folding her hands and bowing her head again had the reverse effect this time. The sun seemed to go behind another cloud as darkness descended once again.

Royce felt a movement beside him as a crystal-clear voice shattered the silence. The solo continued as the sun defeated the clouds and radiated into the cathedral. Gasps were heard as sunlight illuminated the stained-glass windows where the champions of old, the men of renown, were immortalized in the deeds that had won them fame. When the last traces of shadow had fled, the song ended, and Lilith took her place beside Royce.

"Seven, we need seven heads to heal this land," Grammy said, taking her place across from Pomii at the head of the room.

Behind her, Lady Lynn took her place as Royce stood across the aisle behind his brother. Behind him, Citan came as Lilith went to stand behind Lynn. The three remaining houses of the Southern kingdom fell in line accordingly.

"It's no good; we only have six houses represented here," someone muttered. As all turned to the end of those gathered on either side of the aisle, Yao and Cinthia strode forth and joined the nobility.

"Three houses represent the north, three houses represent the south, and a new house represents the kingdom in the center. Let it begin," Grammy said, stamping her staff on the floor.

"WHO CLAIMS THE RIGHT TO UNITE THE LANDS?" a voice boomed across the cathedral.

"I, Royce Sovan, claim the right by taking Lilith as my wife."

"WHO SUPPORTS YOU IN THIS CLAIM?"

"I, Grammy, matriarch of the Zuzax tribe, support their claim."

"I, Lady Lynn, of the House of Sovan, support their claim."

"I, Citan, leader of the merchants guild, support their claim."

"And I, Yao of the Yaoites, support their claim."

"WITH THE JOINING OF THESE FOUR HOUSES BY THESE TWO HERE, THE CURSE IS NOW LIFTED."

An earthquake shook the castle as the northern and southern halves of the island moved toward each other. While all gathered in the cathedral rushed out into the blinding sunlight, a healed land greeted them. Where once the mighty River Wade connected the seas, there flowed a gentle river that anybody could easily cross without the aid of a boat.

"Look!" Lilith said.

The high castle was still surrounded by a waterway but arching that waterway was a bridge made from the boats of all the houses that had brought them to the isle.

Later that evening, after the royal couple had retired to their new chambers, Yao and Citan stood overlooking the setting sun.

"Where will you go now?" Citan asked.

"There is a rebel of a town on the northernmost tip of this island that is calling to me," Yao said with a laugh.

THE END

About the Author

Ben Hall is a writer by day and reader by night. He has authored the St. Noir comic book series that cover the adventures of Captain Cobalt, the Sonic Sleuth and the Mysteries of the Muze.

After serving 8 years with the Marine Corps infantry, Ben continues to utilize those skills and serve his community by volunteering in Search and Rescue. When he isn't out in the Rocky Mountains, Ben enjoys entertaining friends and family with cooking that draws upon his past career as a chef.

You can follow all of his writing adventures at:
www.worldofnom.com